by Jason Finigan

THE KINDRED NOVELS
The Kindred

THE MIXED-ENASSI NOVELS
Destiny's Edge
The Enemy Within

THE KINDRED

JASON FINIGAN

Peregrine

A Peregrine Book

THE KINDRED

ISBN: 978-0-9866951-6-2

PROLOGUE

From the very beginning, the human race has been constantly trying to improve itself, and stumbling many times along the way. Occasionally, though, a discovery is made that is so profound that it changes the human race forever.

Though unfortunately, it is also a sad truth that much of mankind's progress came about as a result of the many wars it has fought during its long, and oft times, bloody history.

By the middle of the twenty-first century, religious fanaticism and extremist terrorist groups had exploded and spread across the globe like a virulent plague threatening to wipe out all life on Earth.

In spite of all of their technological advantages and superior numbers, the governments of the world were not gaining ground against the terrorist groups whose rhetoric appealed to those disenfranchised with their governments' growing inability to protect them. It was quickly decided that a new approach was needed.

Doctor Per Wolff, the foremost leading expert in the field

of genetic engineering, was contacted in the hopes that his research could have military applications. Although his specific interest was in the creation of genetically modified organisms, at the time the laws expressly prohibited him from doing any research with animals other than rodents and other such small creatures. The world was desperate, however, and he was therefore given a special waiver that not only allowed him to work with human subjects—something he had been working toward ever since entering the field—but, in fact, actually mandated it as well.

But although the idea of creating so-called super soldiers capable of finally defeating the terrorist groups intrigued him, he had an altogether, and ultimately more altruistic reason for conducting his research.

His six-year-old son at the time, Lucas, was dying from a rather aggressive form of leukemia which, unfortunately, the doctors had been unsuccessfully treating. The doctors had already determined that it was unlikely Lucas would live past his seventh birthday. It was a prognosis that Doctor Wolff found unacceptable and he refused to give up hope.

Already, his research had produced some startling, but promising, results. Lab rats, afflicted with leukemia, had undergone his DNA splicing procedure, and were now living free of the disease; albeit their appearance had changed slightly as a result. They had grown larger, almost twice their normal size, and the colour of their fur had more red in it.

That is why, when he was approached by the U.N. Security Council to work with them to create their super soldiers, he did not hesitate to accept. He would finally have all the resources necessary to help his son, and failing that, to make sure others in similar situations would not have to suffer the same fate as him.

Doctor Wolff did have one condition prior to accepting to take on the work, though. He told them he wanted Lucas to be his first subject. At first they balked at this condition, decrying the use of his son in his experiments. But he remained insistent, explaining to them his son's dire prognosis. In the end, in their desperation to find a solution for the terrorist threat, they eventually were forced to cave in to his demand.

The research facility where he was to conduct his experiments was located deep underground in an isolated area near Williston Lake in Northern British Columbia, Canada. Security in and around the facility—which had no name—was so tight that no one could get in our out without official clearance. And those that were selected for such clearance were few and far between.

As soon as Doctor Wolff was settled in the new facility, Lucas was transferred from the Garron Family Cancer Centre at Sick Kids hospital in Ottawa, Ontario, where he had been receiving his treatments. The doctors on staff at the facility, which included some of the best cancer care specialists in the world, continued Lucas' treatments there.

In the beginning, Doctor Wolff was singularly focused on ridding his son of the disease that was slowly killing him. His earlier experiments with rats provided him with a place to start. But it was a start only. Based on his extensive research, he knew the key lay in the natural cancer resistance of blind mole rats, the DNA of which he had used successfully in his earlier experiments.

He didn't stop there, however.

Since Lucas would be the first of what he would later call the Kindred, Doctor Wolff knew he had to be especially selective of the traits he wished to enhance, and by how much. Speed, strength, hearing, visual acuity and immunity from disease were all important things to consider, and had to be considered. But he also felt appearance was important as well.

Then, as he watched over his son one night while he peacefully slept for the first time in a long while after receiving the first of several gene re-sequencing treatments, and holding tightly to his chest a plush version of an animal from one of Lucas's favourite cartoon shows on television, an idea suddenly blossomed in Doctor Wolff's mind and a wry grin began to stretch across his weary, unshaven face.

The staff in the facility were very perplexed, and some were even concerned that Doctor Wolff had lost his mind, when the next morning he ordered that DNA samples be collected from foxes, wolves, big cats, bears and even the great apes, and brought to the facility. Lieutenant-General Ben Tate, who oversaw operations at the facility, also questioned Doctor Wolff's unexpected instructions.

Doctor Wolff explained to the General that the terrorists were only successful because they were able to instill fear in people through violence and use that fear to realize their objectives. It was an effective weapon, but one which they, in fact, could use to their advantage by turning that fear back on the terrorists. His idea, then, was to not just enhance the Kindred's natural abilities, but also enhance their appearance as well, making them appear like humanoid versions of some of Earth's most physically intimidating species.

To say that the General liked the idea would have been an understatement, and quickly instructed some of the military personnel in the facility to assist with the collection efforts.

However, because Doctor Wolff was not creating a new organism, rather altering an already existing one, conventional gene re-sequencing techniques alone would not work. That is why he focused on the idea of using nanobots, tiny microscopic robots used primarily for medical purposes to rebuild damaged tissue, to complete the work conventional gene re-sequencing techniques could not accomplish on their own.

He had already begun making the necessary adjustments to the nanobots when the first of the teams sent out to collect the requested DNA returned with their samples. He smiled when he saw the label on the sample it contained.

Before he began the procedure that would turn Lucas into a Kindred, though, Doctor Wolff first discussed it with his son to make sure that it was what he wanted. As it happened Lucas was thrilled with the idea of becoming like one of his favourite cartoon characters. His only worry, and it was a big worry understandably, was that it would hurt. Lucas only agreed to go through with it after Doctor Wolff assured him that while there would be quite a bit of pain, he would do everything possible to make Lucas as comfortable as he could, and promise that when it was done, he would finally be free of his leukemia forever.

In the weeks that followed, Doctor Wolff observed his naked son in the maturation chamber very carefully. Almost for the entire duration Lucas was in the chamber he was unconscious from the sedatives that Doctor Wolff administered.

The maturation chamber was a device of his own design that consisted of a cylindrical glass tank containing billions of his reprogrammed nanobots suspended with Lucas in a warm, nutrient rich, gelatinous fluid that was maintained at a constant temperature. A modified rebreather supplied the oxygen needed for his son to breath while he was submerged in the fluid.

Changes in Lucas began to happen almost immediately, and at a very rapid rate. Every day saw new changes in the boy. A dense coat of soft, silky and relatively long bright reddish-rusty coloured fur with yellowish tints was beginning to grow on his body until soon every part of him was covered in it. At the same time his fur grew in, his body also began to change shape. First, his mouth and nose grew outward, forming a short muzzle that revealed two lines of sharp, pointed teeth. The ears drew back slightly until they were pointed and erect. His arms and legs became long, thin and sleek looking, and his hands and feet turned into large paws with clawed fingers. Additionally, Lucas also began growing in a long, bushy white-tipped tail at the base of his spine.

When the transformation was finally completed, Lucas emerged from the maturation chamber, unconscious still, but now looking nothing like his human self any more. Instead, he looked more like a humanoid version of a red fox, and except for the colouring, very similar to the character Lucas loved so much.

When Lucas eventually woke up, laying in his bed in the facility, he looked up at his father with his new light-gold coloured eyes and smiled.

The first of the Kindred was born.

Testing to determine Lucas's new enhanced abilities began soon after Doctor Wolff determined that Lucas had sufficiently recovered from his ordeal, the preliminary results of which, as submitted to General Tate in his report, were promising.

Subject has been responding remarkably well to the treatments; much better than initially hoped. He shows no signs that he is rejecting the genetic re-sequencing. Bone growth and muscle density have increased two-fold.

Visual acuity tests suggest that impaired vision at early stages of development previously reported have resolved on their own without intervention. Subject now possesses a visual acuity that is on par with, and may even surpass, that of humans. He appears to have retained the ability to see in near total darkness due to the presence of a tapetum lucidum behind the retina.

The subject's hearing is extremely acute, and is now able to perceive up to sixty-five thousand Hertz of sound at ranges of up to one-hundred sixty feet.

Motor coordination skills and muscle reflexes far surpasses expectations, and testing on the obstacle course shows marked improvement on an almost daily basis. It was suggested by Doctor Vasquez that we proceed to phase two of our testing, ahead of schedule.

General Tate was so impressed with the results that he wasted no time ordering Doctor Wolff to begin creating new Kindred. To that end, Doctor Wolff informed the General he would need military personnel to volunteer to undergo the procedure, preferably ones who have been critically wounded or who have a terminal illness and therefore had little to lose by becoming Kindred. However, he also cautioned that each of the potential candidates should first be required to undergo a thorough psychological screening before being considered. This was to ensure that any of the Kindred born would not later pose a threat to humanity.

But when the General then expressed a desire to begin putting Lucas through the same rigorous training as the rest of the Kindred, Doctor Tate emphatically refused. Under no circumstances would he allow his son to be turned into a soldier, especially not since Lucas was still only a six-year-old child, no matter that he had experienced significant growth while changing.

Doctor Wolff was ultimately successful in convincing the U.N. Security Council not to force his son to undergo such intensive training, overturning General Tate's orders. It was not as difficult a task as he expected, though, since the U.N. Security Council had never been comfortable with allowing Lucas to become a Kindred in the first place. Still, the Council did encourage Doctor Wolff to allow Lucas to undergo a less intensive training regimen in order to learn self defence techniques and to help him better understand and control his new abilities. He had no objections to this.

By the time the existence of the Kindred was made public, several thousand of them had already been born, and already were quite effectively fighting against the terrorist forces across the globe. For the very first time ever, it was the terrorists who were afraid as they were systematically hunted down and confronted with the angry, snarling faces of the Kindred bearing down on them with their teeth bared and their claws extended. The Kindred had no need for weapons of any kind. Their own natural abilities were more than sufficient.

During this period, the U.N. enacted a law which prohibited any citizen from belonging to, or organizing, any non-registered religious or political group, making it near impossible for another terrorist group to form.

The first of the Kindred to be born were created with love and delicate care under Doctor Wolff's direction. But out of all of them, it was Lucas he was the most proud of. Such was the care he put into them that the Kindred are now considered by many, even among the human population, to be quite attractive. They are also quite happy to be what they are. Some of the

Kindred have even begun to form lasting, loving bonds with human partners.

No one could quite appreciate the full implications of Doctor Wolff's work until it was discovered that the Kindred, besides being excellent fighters and beautiful people, had also apparently retained the ability to procreate. What made this even more remarkable was the fact that the Kindred could not only produce offspring with other Kindred, but with humans as well. The Kindred genes were dominant, though, so any pairing between a Kindred and a Human would almost always result in the birth of another Kindred.

It was because of this ability that some people became somewhat resentful of the Kindred. They feared that one day the Kindred would become the dominant species on the planet, replacing mankind. Out of this fear was born new laws which effectively relegated the Kindred to second-class citizenship. Unbeknownst to many, though, Doctor Wolff secretly believed, and hoped, that the Kindred—really his Kindred—through breeding with humans would eventually become the next step in the human race's evolution.

Although understandably anxious during this period of uncertainty, as prejudice and violence against the Kindred was not unheard of, and in some parts of the world were increasingly frequent, the Kindred could afford to be patient. One of the many gifts given to them by Doctor Wolff was an extremely low metabolism rate that, coupled with other factors, enabled them to live longer natural lives than humans. Lucas, who was the first, almost thirty years after becoming a Kindred had aged so slowly that physically he still looked quite young and could easily be mistaken for a teenager. At times, it was observed, he often acted like one as well.

It took decades for the laws to finally be changed, during

which time the legal status of the Kindred was confused. Laws were passed only to be revoked months later, and then later reintroduced as new administrations came into power. But eventually, after a long and sometimes painful wait, the Kindred were finally recognized by the World Court as persons under the law.

ONE

ucas Wolff walked along the banks of the Fraser River, alone but content. He preferred it this way. It was on nights like this that he felt the most at peace, far from the noise and the heavy nauseating smells of the city that constantly assailed his senses when he was there. This is why he rarely entered the city if he could avoid it.

But out here in the peace and quiet of nature, at night and with the almost full mooning shining down on him, lighting his way, he was free to run, to hunt, and to think.

Not that he needed the moon to see, for he had walked this particular route many times before and knew it well.

A cool breeze blew across the river past him. The coolness of it didn't bother him, though, like it would most humans. He was, after all, Kindred—part human, part red fox—so the cold never bothered him. In fact, he preferred it over the hot summer sun. Like a red fox his winter coat would shed as the seasons changed and his summer coat grew in. It was much shorter and allowed his skin to breathe much easier.

Lucas eventually came upon a steep embankment rising up from the side of the riverbed, tall grasses and thick bushes growing from it. Had he been human, it would have proved a formidable obstacle and he likely would have opted to travel around to less treacherous terrain. As it was, though, Lucas's strong, slender legs and his nimble agility enabled him to scale the embankment with relative ease.

It was atop the embankment that he found himself on an old dirt trail leading to a narrow, but long, foot bridge that connected the two sides of the river. Of course he had been here before, and crossed the bridge many times, just as he was about to, but then something unexpected caught his attention.

Thanks to his keen eyesight, a gift from the red fox half of him, he was clearly able to discern the shape of a young human male sitting on the bridge railing, his legs dangling over the edge. His head was bowed, as though looking intently into the dark, fast moving waters far below, and as Lucas cautiously approached the male, he could now hear the faintest sounds of heavy sobs coming from the boy. He was crying.

Lucas's movements alerted the boy to his presence and he lifted his tear streaked face to look at him, an alarmed expression on his face.

"Don't come any closer," the boy cried frightfully.

Lucas stopped in his tracks. He was close enough now, though that he could clearly make out the boy's features. And it was indeed a boy, probably no older than sixteen or seventeen years of age. To Lucas's shock the boy was incredibly thin and frail looking as though he had not eaten in days; or perhaps longer. The telltale signs of a dire illness were borne all over his pale, sunken in face.

Despite the obvious illness that afflicted the boy's frail

body, Lucas decided he was otherwise a very nice looking young man. His eyes were a brilliant light blue that shown brightly like oysters in the pale moon light, his golden hued blonde hair was cut short, almost military style, and even though he obviously was physically very weak, Lucas instantly saw a strength within him that he was instantly attracted to. This boy had clearly suffered much in his young life, much more than anyone his age should ever have to. But now it had appeared he had reached the end of his rope. As brave as he was, he could fight no longer.

The way the boy was sitting, perched atop the railing and looking down at the rolling waters far beneath them, it was not all that difficult to guess what the boy's intentions were.

"Please don't," Lucas said, quietly, pleading with the boy. "Whatever it is, it can be worked out."

"No it can't!" the boy screamed back at him with such force that it momentarily startled Lucas. "No one can make it better," the boy said in a calmer, almost whispered voice as he looked back down to the water.

Lucas could see that he was getting ready to jump. He dared to take another step towards the boy.

"I'd like to try, if you'll let me," Lucas said in as soft a voice as he could.

This time the boy barked out a laugh, looking back at Lucas incredulously.

"No one can help me. The doctors said so!"

The tears then suddenly began to flow again, streaking slowly down his already moist cheeks.

"What's wrong?" Lucas asked gently.

"AIDS," the boy said simply in a low voice that was barely more than a whisper.

Suddenly it all made perfect sense to Lucas; the boy's frail appearance and his willingness, no, his desperate need, to end his own life as the hopelessness of his crisis completely overwhelmed him.

"The meds won't work on me any more," the boy continued.

"I'm sorry," Lucas said, with genuine sorrow in his voice.

"My own mom doesn't want anything to do with me any more. She hates me."

"I'm sure that's not true," Lucas said, his head shaking emphatically in disbelief.

He had managed to move up beside the boy now and sit down with him, just as the boy was.

"The last thing she said to me before kicking me out was that she didn't need a dirty, diseased little faggot polluting her house." The boy said with as much vehemence he could muster.

By then he was once again wracked by terrible heaving sobs as all his emotions poured out of him all at once.

A flash of anger crossed across Lucas's face, his once erect ears folded flat against his skull, disappearing within his long fur, and his tail flicking under him in agitation.

He pulled the boy to him as the boy continued to cry his pain and grief out. After a few minutes his sobs eventually lessened and then stopped altogether. He sat up and looked up at Lucas, who, even when sitting, towered over the smaller boy.

"I'm sorry, I got your fur all wet," he said, flushing slightly.

Lucas chuckled with amusement that the boy, despite everything he has been through, could suddenly become so embarrassed by as simple a thing as getting his fur wet.

"I'd still like to help if you'll let me," he said after calming down, but still smiling.

Hope flashed in the boy's eyes for just a moment, but

then disappeared just as quickly.

"It's impossible," he said sadly.

Lucas, however, was not about to give up hope. He didn't even know why he felt so compelled to save him. He didn't even know the boy. But at the same time he couldn't deny that he quickly found himself inexplicably being drawn to this boy as though he had always been meant to find him at this exact moment to save him.

"What's your name?" Lucas asked.

"Elijah," the boy said quietly. "Elijah Saunders."

"Well, Elijah, I'm Lucas Wolff."

The boy, Elijah, gasped, his eyes opening wide in recognition. Everyone knew that name, because everyone also knew that Lucas was the first of the Kindred to ever be born.

"Come on, let me take you to my home so you can rest," Lucas suggested to the still bewildered boy.

Slowly, Elijah nodded and allowed himself to be led off the bridge. He was so weak he had to be supported by Lucas who put an arm around him to hold him up.

Elijah was not only impressed with Lucas's strength, as he effortlessly walked him off the bridge and onto the dirt path, but also by his incredible gentleness as he held him. With a tired sigh he leaned into the Kindred, enjoying the comforting warmth of his long, soft fur.

He did not have much experience with the Kindred, his mother had expressly forbade him from ever associating with their "kind," as she put it, even though he was classmates with several. Such was her hatred of them she always referred to the Kindred derisively as beasts or other less than polite names. He tried to ignore her when she started on one of her rants about the Kindred. A difficult thing to do when she's in the same room and yelling at the top of her lungs; usually directing her vitriol at the television while the news was on.

As much as she hated the Kindred, though, it paled in comparison to her hatred of people who were gay.

He had known he was gay since he was very young, though at that age he had no concept of what it meant to be gay. He just knew he was different than the other boys in his class at school, and his friends.

Growing up with his mother, and knowing her hatred of gays, who she often called faggots, he had to keep that part of him hidden from her. She had a terrible temper, and often blew at the slightest of perceived provocations. On many occasions— too numerous to count—he found himself on the receiving end of one of her outbursts. He feared her more than anything else, even death.

The coolness of the night air caused him to shiver and almost instinctively press himself further into Lucas's fur, as though trying to bury himself within it. Lucas simply smiled and held onto Elijah more tightly when he did.

But it pretty soon became apparent that Elijah was getting weaker with every step. He suddenly tripped and nearly fell, and would have, had Lucas not been helping him. Growing very concerned, Lucas suggested that he carry him the rest of the way. Poor Elijah was in no state to mount any kind of protest, and he knew it. He nodded his assent and then was swiftly hoisted up into Lucas's arms as effortlessly as if Lucas had been picking up a piece of paper. Again Elijah was impressed with the Kindred's strength, even in the semi-delirious state he was in.

Once again Lucas set off, this time with Elijah held close to his chest. Somewhere along the way, though, he noticed that Elijah had slipped into unconsciousness and his skin was now covered in a light film of sweat indicating he had become feverish. Cursing under his breath, he picked up the pace. If he didn't hurry, Lucas knew his new-found friend probably wouldn't make it through the night, he was that ill.

All of a sudden, the need to get Elijah the help he so desperately needed became a whole lot more urgent. Lucas quickly draped the unconscious boy over his back as he dropped to all fours. As soon as he was assured that Elijah would not slip off, he then made a mad dash through the forest. The boy's weight did not slow him in the slightest as he effortlessly raced past the trees and bushes until he broke out of the forest and onto a dark and deserted road. He knew the road led into the city, though, following it as fast as he could run.

He must have looked a sight as he entered the city with Elijah hung over his back. But he ignored the alarmed stares he received and turned down the main boulevard that would take him to where he knew help for Elijah could be found. The doctors Elijah had seen may not have believed anything more could be done for the boy, but he was hopeful there was one person who could do something to help him, if there was time.

Stopping at the door to the large residence at the end of the street, he didn't bother knocking but instead pushed his way inside by slamming his shoulder against the door, his strength such that the simple metal latch that held the door closed was no match for him. It broke easily under the strain.

His noisy arrival did not go unnoticed. An elderly man quickly ran into the main foyer to see what all the racket was about. When he did, he stopped with a start when he saw Lucas standing there, his fur matted with sweat and holding in his arms an unconscious Elijah.

"Lucas, just what in the name of God is going on here?" he asked. Despite the alarming sight before him his voice was surprisingly even.

"Dad, he needs your help," Lucas said.

Doctor Per Wolff was still a very attractive man at the ripe old age—as he put it—of sixty-seven. Now long since retired he had settled down into a part-time teaching position at the Vancouver campus of the University of British Columbia. When not teaching, though, he spent most of his time at his large estate in the city of Surrey.

He was a fairly tall man, almost as tall as Lucas was, with short mostly white hair that he kept neat. He was still in fairly good shape, with a toned and strong physique that was easily seen under his night clothes that he had hastily put on.

His eyes quickly focused on the boy in Lucas's arms. He took a step toward them.

"What's wrong with the boy?" he asked, eyeing the boy carefully.

Quickly Lucas explained the situation to his father, telling him of his meeting with Elijah on the bridge, the boy's intentions to commit suicide and learning that he had AIDS and had recently been kicked out of his house.

"He was getting weaker and weaker until he just faded out in my arms. Can you help him please, Dad?"

Per could see the sadness in his son's eyes. Of course he knew of his son's gentle and caring spirit, and knew he would have asked the same of him if it were any other living being. But there was something more in Lucas's eyes when he looked down at the stricken boy in his arms, a longing that he had never seen in his son before.

"Bring him upstairs, Lucas," he instructed calmly, turning and heading up the wide staircase himself.

Per led Lucas to his private lab, located on the second floor, where he preferred to work when doing new research as opposed to the labs offered by the University. He had always felt more comfortable working alone, without anyone constantly peering over his shoulder.

The lab was large and stark and so much different from the rest of the house. Stainless steel shelves and tables along the walls shimmered icily, which seemed to take all the warmth out of the room and causing Lucas to shiver involuntarily even though he was, in fact, quite warm. He always hated the effect the lab had on him. Lab equipment of all sorts was dispersed seemingly at random throughout the room. Lucas knew better, however. His father was a very particular man and everything in his lab was precisely where it was meant to be. Piercingly bright circles from the lights above the examination table in the centre of the room made the rest of the room appear shaded. They were much too bright for Lucas's liking.

Lucas gently set Elijah down on the examination table as directed by his father. As soon as he did, the table's diagnostic computer instantly activated and a life-sized three dimensional anatomical image of Elijah that was slightly translucent appeared approximately two metres above him. Lucas could see all of Elijah's internal organs, and also the extent of the damage his disease had caused.

Per approached the table, a data pad in his hands.

"He said the doctors told him the retroviral drugs they normally would use can't help him any more," Lucas said quietly, unable to take his eyes off of Lucas.

Per nodded gravely.

"He's dying, there's no doubt about it," he said with a bit of sadness in his voice. "Without treatment he won't live more than a day, probably less."

"Is there anything you can do for him?"

"His disease has progressed to the point where his internal organs are beginning to shut down."

"Please, Dad, if there's even the slightest chance he can

be saved..." His voice trailed off as tears of desperation began welling up in his eyes.

Per's eyes narrowed at this unexpected display of raw emotion from his son. Appearing to come to a decision, he nodded his head slowly.

"I suppose asking you to wait outside would be pointless."

"I want to help," Lucas nodded, with a wide elated smile.

"Then get me the nano-energizer please, Lucas," Per instructed him, noisily cracking his knuckles as he usually did when he was about to get to work on a project. "It looks like this is going to be a long night."

The rising morning sun filtered through the gap in the curtains of the partially open bedroom window, the light falling on the youth sleeping peacefully on the bed like multihued rays of gold descending from the sky. A gentle breeze blew into the room, filling it with the scent of fresh spring air.

The boy stirred, slowly rousing from a deep, restful sleep, the first he could remember having in a long time. He could feel the warmth of the blanket that covered him and the soft mattress that supported him. It was a welcome change from the hard unyielding ground he had been forced to sleep on since being kicked out of his mother's house.

Elijah's tousled haired head shot up with a start and he peered over with bleary heavy lidded eyes at Lucas who was clad only in a pair of tight fighting shorts and was sitting in the shadows beside the bed, watching him.

"Then it wasn't a dream," Elijah said quietly, his throat sounding hoarse.

"No, it wasn't a dream." Lucas answered.

He got up from his chair to pour Elijah a glass of ice-cold water from a pitcher on the nightstand beside him.

Elijah accepted the water gratefully as he groggily sat up to drink it.

"How do you feel?" Lucas asked.

"Better," Elijah said. His eyes flew open with surprise when he suddenly realized that he did indeed feel better. Much better than he had felt in ages.

An amused grin tugged at the corner of Lucas's lips at Elijah's sudden realization.

"How?" Elijah asked quietly as bewildered tears of immense joy and relief filled his eyes.

"When you fell unconscious, I brought you to my father's home. He has a lab here and was able to repair some of the damage that had been caused by your illness."

"But the doctors said nothing could be done—"

Lucas interrupted him with a roaring laugh.

"My father has never cared much for the opinions of doctors, Elijah. I wouldn't be alive today if he did."

Of course Elijah knew what Lucas was referring to. Every child who ever attended elementary school knew of the history of the Kindred and how Doctor Wolff came to create them starting with his young son who at the time was terminally ill with leukemia.

"Does that mean your father has somehow cured me?" he asked in a small hopeful voice.

"Not quite," Lucas said, causing Elijah's heart to sink. "But my father has given you a small army of nanobots which are even now searching for, and destroying, any genetic material that does not contain your DNA," Lucas added quickly.

"How long have I been here?"

"You were in the maturation chamber for two days, and

you've been asleep for an additional three."

Elijah's eyes opened wide with surprise again.

"Have you been sitting there this whole time, then?"

Lucas smiled warmly, his ears giving a tiny flick.

"Mostly. I wanted to be here in case you woke up," he said.

"Thank you," Elijah said quietly.

"Are you hungry?"

Before Elijah could respond, though, his stomached answered for him, loud enough that Lucas had no difficulty hearing it.

"I'll take that as a yes," Lucas laughed.

With a wide grin, Elijah threw off his blanket when he suddenly discovered, to his shock, that he had been naked underneath the covers the whole time and was now inadvertently giving Lucas an unobstructed view of him.

Lucas's ears pricked up noticeably right away, a thin smile tugging at the corners of his lips as he gazed approvingly at the sight before him.

Blushing furiously, which Lucas found extremely cute, Elijah quickly pulled the blanket back over him in embarrassment, and holding it close to his body.

"Where are my clothes?" he asked.

Lucas—with a smile still on his face—responded by tipping his head towards a chair by the wall on the opposite side of the bed where a neat bundle of folded clothes lay.

"I'll leave you to get dressed," Lucas said, standing back up. "When you're ready you can come downstairs and join us for some breakfast."

"Thanks again, Lucas. I promise I'll pay you back for everything you and your father have done for me somehow."

"Don't worry about it," Lucas said, with a dismissive

wave of his hand and another wide smile. "I'm just glad you're feeling better."

Lucas then turned and left the room, closing the door quietly behind him, leaving a completely bewildered Elijah staring after him.

Was he actually checking me out just then? Elijah wondered as he got out of bed to get dressed.

He all of a sudden felt a familiar stirring between his legs. Looking down he could see that at least one part of him liked the idea.

TWO

Lucas was waiting for Elijah at the foot of the stairs when he saw him beginning to descend at last, looking much rested and practically glowing with happiness. When Elijah reached the bottom of the stairs he surprised Lucas by wrapping his arms around him in a warm, lingering embrace. Lucas returned the hug, happily, nuzzling his neck and taking in his scent.

Elijah looked up at him when they separated, with a wide grin on his face.

"I wanted to do that when you were upstairs to properly thank you for all you've done for me," he said. "But I wasn't exactly dressed for it at the time, though, and I didn't think you'd appreciate suddenly being hugged by a naked seventeen-year-old boy who you'd only just met."

Lucas laughed.

"I really wouldn't have minded at all, Elijah," he said quietly.

"You're gay, aren't you?" Elijah said.

"Was it that obvious?"

"Only a little."

With another laugh, Lucas put an arm around Elijah's shoulders.

"Come on, it's time for breakfast and we don't want to let it get cold. My father hates cold eggs."

Lucas guided Elijah into the kitchen where his father was busy spreading butter on some toast. He heard them enter, and turned, smiling when he saw Elijah.

"Well you are looking much better, young man."

"Thanks to you, I'm told, sir," Elijah said. "Thank you."

"Please have a seat. Breakfast will be ready in a minute," Per said and went back to finish buttering the toast.

Lucas and Elijah sat down at the round wooden kitchen table which Lucas had already set earlier. Elijah thought it odd that Lucas had purposefully picked the seat directly in front of the window so he was facing away from it, and the bright sunlight that shone into the room.

"The bright light hurts my eyes," Lucas said as though reading Elijah's thoughts.

"Sorry, I didn't know."

"I've always been sensitive to bright lights, ever since I was little, and still human."

"Lucas spent much of his youth in one hospital or another, where the lights there are too harsh," Per said, arriving at the table with a stack of buttered toast, a wood basket lined with paper towel and filled with crisp bacon, and a metal bowl filled with scrambled eggs.

Per caught Elijah eyeing the food in anticipation and smiled.

"We don't wait on ceremony in this house, son. So go

ahead and dig," he said.

Again Elijah blushed in that cute way Lucas loved so much and began helping himself to a bit of everything, piling it on his plate. It was probably more than he could eat, but it all looked so good that he couldn't resist.

They ate mostly in silence, and except for the sounds of utensils being scraped against plates and the occasional bird singing outside, not another sound could be heard throughout the house. It was the most at peace Elijah had felt in a long while.

Finishing his breakfast, and feeling quite full, Per pushed his empty plate away from him.

"Lucas tells me you had been kicked out of your house by your mother. Is this true?" he asked.

Elijah nodded as he finished off the last piece of bacon on his plate.

"When she found out that I was gay and was HIV positive, she freaked out. She started yelling and physically pushed me out the door before throwing all of my clothes at me, no matter if they were clean or dirty, and then told me to never come back."

There were tears once again welling up in Elijah's eyes as he recalled the events that led him to being forced out onto the streets. Even with how his mother treated him he still loved her, and it hurt him so much that she had rejected him like that.

Lucas reached over and tenderly put a hand over his.

"I'm sorry your mom couldn't accept you for who you are, Elijah. I really think you're an amazing guy and she's a fool for letting you go like that," Lucas said.

Elijah couldn't help himself as he blushed a deep crimson colour, feeling embarrassed by Lucas's praise of him. He was not used to anyone complimenting him like that. But it felt good, especially coming from him.

Per leaned back in his chair, its soft creaking under Per's weight drawing their attention to him.

"After Lucas became Kindred and was cured of his leukemia, I'm afraid I stopped paying attention to him as much as I should have. My work, unfortunately, consumed most of my time," he said slowly, as though trying to choose his words carefully.

"You were always there for me when I needed you, though, Dad," Lucas interrupted, which earned him a reproving glare from his father.

"So when he came out to me almost twenty years ago," Per continued. "I'd realized that without intending to, I'd pushed him almost completely out of my life. After the shock of it wore off, I did the only thing I could think of. I grabbed him into a tight hug and told him how much I loved him. From that point on I made it my priority to be as involved in his life as I had been when he was real young."

"You made me so proud to be your son that day, Dad."

"I wish my mom could have been more like you, Doctor Wolff," Elijah said quietly.

"I am very surprised that in this day and age anyone still harboured such homophobic attitudes," Per said.

"I know. None of my friends or their families has a problem with me being gay. They all keep asking when I'm going to get a boyfriend."

"Has your mom always been like this?"

"She wasn't when my Mom and Dad were together. At least, I never heard her say anything bad about gays or the Kindred. She was always so nice and caring with me. We always used to have so much fun playing when I was a kid."

"What happened to your father?"

"One day before I turned ten, he disappeared and never

came back. Mom told me that he fell in love with a Kindred—A male. He now lives somewhere in Ottawa. Sometimes he sends me money to help with school and on my birthdays."

"And when your mother discovered you were gay—"

"I guess she thought I was betraying her like my Dad did," Elijah finished. The tears that had been welling up in his eyes began to fall. "But I didn't mean to be gay. I really didn't."

Suddenly it was as though a dam had burst and all of his pent up emotions came suddenly pouring out of him all at once in deep heaving sobs.

Lucas stood up from his chair and pulled Elijah up into a comforting embrace. He held him close as this boy who had suffered so much in his short life cried his heart out. Once again, Lucas noticed, his fur was getting wet. But he didn't care. He just continued to hold Elijah.

"It's going to be okay, Elijah," he promised quietly into his ear. "You're with me now, and I'm not going to let anyone else hurt you."

Elijah managed to get his sobs under control and he lifted his head up from Lucas's chest to look up at him with tear stained eyes, a hopeful expression on his face.

"I just found you. Do you think I'm just going to let you slip away from me that easily?" Lucas continued softly.

"That sounds almost like a proposition," Elijah said, managing a fleeting wry grin.

"Would you be upset if it was?"

"No, I'd be flattered, and really happy that you like me."

Per sat in his chair watching the exchange, shaking his head in bewilderment as he realized that a very close, very special bond was forming between them right before his eyes.

"My son. He may be thirty-two-years-old, but he's still very much a teenager. Always thinking with his heart," he muttered quietly to himself.

"I heard that," Lucas said, sharply turning his head to look at his father.

"Blasted Kindred hearing!" Per said with mock indignation, causing both Elijah and Lucas to laugh hysterically.

When they had settled down, they began gathering up their dishes to put into the dishwasher.

"So where were you staying before I found you?" Lucas asked.

"At a friends house," Elijah said.

"Well then, the first order of business, after we're finished here, is for you to call to let your friend know that you are alright," Per suggested. "I'm sure your friend is probably worried about not hearing from you."

Elijah nodded in agreement.

"I can't go back there, though. His parents would only allow me to stay the one night."

"Where do you go to school?" Per asked.

"Fraser Heights Secondary School."

"Really?" Lucas said, his ears pricking up at once. "That's only a few blocks from where my apartment is."

Elijah cocked his head on one side with a slight frown as he looked at Lucas quizzically.

"I thought you lived here," he said.

"I just keep the apartment for when I want some private time," Lucas said, shaking his head. "But I spend most of my time here with Dad, or at the university when he's teaching."

When the last of the dishes were put away in the dishwasher, Lucas beckoned Elijah to follow him to the phone where he could call his friend.

As Elijah followed Lucas out of the kitchen, though, he suddenly found himself completely captivated with Lucas's bushy, white-tipped tail which stuck out from an opening in his shorts. His eyes closely followed it as it swayed back and forth almost hypnotically behind the Kindred. At that moment Elijah decided it was the most sexy sight he had ever laid eyes on. He was so distracted by it, in fact, that he almost ran into the back of Lucas, not realizing that he had stopped.

"Sorry," Elijah said,

Lucas just smiled at him as he showed him the video phone sitting on a small table by the staircase.

Does he have any clue what he's doing to me? Elijah wondered.

Kenneth Hamilton was packing his lunch into his backpack, getting ready for another day of school, when the phone on the counter all of a sudden began to ring. It startled him and caused him to drop his apple which rolled off the kitchen table and landed with a resounding thud on he ceramic tile floor. It did not even bounce once.

Ignoring the apple, which he figured was probably badly bruised and not worth eating now, he reached for the connect button.

"Hello?" he said.

His eyes opened wide with relief and happiness when he saw the image of Elijah appear on the phone's screen. He didn't recognize the number, displayed at the bottom of the screen, but that didn't matter to him.

"Mom, come quick, Elijah's on the phone!" he called out excitedly.

She could be heard rushing from her room upstairs, followed by quick footsteps racing down the stairs.

"Elijah, where are you, man? Are you alright?" Kenneth

asked as his mother hurried into the kitchen, hastily dressed and wearing a very relieved expression.

"I'm okay now, Ken," Elijah's voice assured them.

Indeed, he even sounded better to Kenneth, much better than he did on the day he disappeared.

"I met someone a few nights ago and he's been taking care of me," Elijah continued.

"Mom and I were really worried about you. You didn't do anything crazy, did you?"

Elijah paused for a moment, and then with a sad expression slowly nodded.

"Let me talk to him," Kenneth's mother said.

"Elijah, honey, where are you calling from. We can come and get you. Your things are still here."

"You're not going to believe this but I'm actually at Doctor Wolff's house, and I'm here with him and Lucas," Elijah said, with a wide grin.

"No way!" Kenneth exclaimed. "Oh man, you are so lucky."

Just then a large fox-like Kindred with long bright reddish-rusty coloured fur, except under his chin, chest and stomach, which was mostly white, joined Elijah on the screen.

"Hello, Ken. I'm Lucas. It's nice to meet you."

Kenneth was completely speechless. Never in a million years did he think he would ever be talking to Lucas, the first Kindred ever to be born.

"Hello, Lucas. I'm Alayna Hamilton, Ken's mother."

"Hello, Mrs. Hamilton," Lucas said with an acknowledging flick of his ears.

"Please, just Alayna," she said, smiling at his formality.

"No, I don't think my dad would let me," Lucas said with a playful grin.

"You're darn right I wouldn't!" came a disembodied voice over the phone, startling Kenneth and Alayna, but causing both Lucas and Elijah to snicker openly.

"You don't have to trouble yourself by coming to pick Elijah up. He still needs to rest for a bit until my dad says it's okay for him to go back to school," Lucas said.

"But I would really appreciate it if I could get my clothes, please," Elijah added.

"So what did happen to you? Why did you disappear like that?" Kenneth asked.

Elijah looked a little uncomfortable until Lucas gave him an encouraging flick of his ears.

"After school I left and wandered a bit until I found myself on that foot bridge over the river. The meds weren't working, and I was getting really weak. I decided I didn't want to end up like those other AIDS patients, basically bedridden and wasting away until I died from one stupid bacteria or another. I was going to jump and let the river take me, and be finally at peace. But that's when Lucas showed up and stopped me."

Kenneth and Alayna both gasped in shock. They, of course, knew Elijah had been depressed about his AIDS, but neither of them had any clue that he had been so despondent that he had been considering taking his own life.

"Elijah, dear, you should have told us. We would have figured something out," she said quietly.

Elijah shook his head.

"There was nothing you could have done, Mrs. Hamilton, and I didn't want you to see me like that."

Kenneth knew he was right, but it still hurt to think that he could have lost the best friend he ever had. They had been so close they were like brothers.

"But you're looking so much better now, you're alright

aren't you?" he asked.

"After I found him I brought him to my dad's house where he was able to stabilize Elijah. He now has an army's worth of nanobots hunting down and destroying all traces of the HIV," Lucas explained.

"Your father was able to cure his AIDS?" Kenneth asked, his eyes opening wide in amazement.

"For the most part," Lucas nodded. "But it takes time for the nanobots to do their work and the virus is very quick to mutate. That's why Elijah has to remain as stress free as possible to better enable the nanobots to do their work. It's sort of the same thing my dad did with me when he cured my leukemia, only less drastic since this won't change Elijah into a Kindred."

"I don't know how we can ever thank you, Lucas, for all that you and your father have done for him. Kenneth was really worried when Elijah never came back from school."

"I'm sorry, Ken, I just didn't know if I could have gone through with it if I saw your face, so I had to leave. I didn't mean to hurt you," Elijah said.

"It's okay, buddy. I'm glad you're safe," Kenneth assured him. "I'd like to see you though, after school, if I can."

"No, I think you should go to him now, Kenneth," Alayna said.

"Mom?" Kenneth said, disbelieving what he had just heard. Did his mother really just suggest that he skip school?

"I'll call your school to tell them that there has been a family emergency, and you won't be in today," she said. "The two of you are like brothers. Go see him."

"Thanks, Mom!" Kenneth exclaimed loudly, grabbing his mother in a very grateful embrace.

He let her go quickly, though, when he remembered that they were still in the middle of a phone call and Elijah and Lucas were watching.

"But this is an exception, not the rule," Alayna cautioned him. She was flushed slightly from her son's sudden embrace, something he rarely did since becoming a teenager. "And I will be collecting your school work on the way back from work for you to do," she finished.

Kenneth quickly sobered up, nodding his head in understanding.

"Yes, ma'am," he said, though with a wide grin when he said it.

"I'll give you the address," Lucas said.

THREE

Kenneth drove up the long, narrow driveway, past the open wrought-iron gates that bordered the home's property and into the small courtyard. Parked to one side, just outside a detached garage, sat parked an older, but well maintained, E-Car.

E-Cars had become extremely popular in recent years as the price of gasoline rose to astronomical levels and most families could no longer afford using their internal combustion engine driven automobiles. They were quickly replaced with all-electric vehicles. Most roadways, once paved with asphalt, were now covered with solar road panels, which harvest the energy of the sun to provide power for the cities, and also to charge all-electric vehicles' batteries while they were being driven.

As Kenneth slowly rolled up alongside the parked E-Car, he had the opportunity to get a good look of Doctor Wolff's house. It was of modest size, which surprised him, considering he expected something much grander than the two level brick home before him. It was an old home, though in remarkably good shape, with a steep pitched roof and old-style shutters and windows painted brown that made it look very inviting.

Getting out of his car, and grabbing the duffel bag containing Elijah's clothes from the trunk of his car, he approached the front door where he located the antique style pull chain type door ringer. Curiously, the latch on the door looked brand new, as though it had recently been replaced. He pulled on the chain and could clearly hear from inside the muffled echoing sound of a bell ringing throughout the house.

The door swung open, and he was immediately met with the smiling, excited face of Elijah, who quickly stepped outside to embrace him in a tight, lingering hug.

"Hey, buddy," Kenneth said softly into Elijah's ear as he returned the hug.

Elijah still looked as thin and frail as he remembered when he last saw him, but there was a renewed strength within him he could tell, especially by the way he was holding onto him so tightly as though afraid of letting him go.

Lucas appeared in the doorway and smiled as the two friends were reunited.

"Welcome to Wolff house, Kenneth," he said.

The two boys reluctantly released each other and Kenneth walked up to Lucas to shake his hand.

"Thanks, Lucas. It's quite the place you have here."

Lucas shrugged his shoulders in a typically human fashion.

"It's quiet, which I prefer," he said. "The city can be so noisy sometimes."

Kenneth nodded in agreement.

"I hear you."

Lucas led them into the house, Kenneth staring in awe at

the remarkable craftsmanship that was inside, and into the living room. No sooner had they all taken seats when Doctor Wolff entered the room carrying a tray containing several glasses filled with tomato juice.

Doctor Wolff caught Kenneth's perplexed expression and smiled knowingly.

"Elijah needs to build up his strength and it would be unfair if everyone else was drinking something he couldn't," he explained.

"Really, I don't mind," Elijah said, gratefully accepting his glass of tomato juice from Doctor Wolff.

"It's okay, I like the stuff any way," Kenneth said.

"So how long have you and Elijah been friends, Kenneth?" Lucas asked when his father left the room, leaving the three of them to get acquainted, or reacquainted in Elijah and Kenneth's case.

"Please, call me Ken. All my friends do," Kenneth said. "Elijah and I have known each other since we were very little, actually. We pretty much grew up together."

"Yeah, except for last year when your family temporarily moved to Toronto because of your father's job," Elijah said.

"But we still stayed in touch regularly by email. That's how I learned that he had been diagnosed as being HIV positive."

"And that he was gay?" Lucas asked.

Kenneth laughed.

"I already knew that a long time ago. He came out to me when he was only twelve."

"I remember I was so afraid then that you wouldn't like me anymore. I almost didn't."

"I still would have gotten it out of you eventually anyway, though," Kenneth said.

Elijah smiled, and blushed weakly.

God he's so cute when he blushes like that, Lucas thought.

"Yeah, but don't forget it was me who got you together with Suzi," Elijah reminded him.

"Who's that, your girlfriend?" Lucas asked Kenneth.

Kenneth nodded, a wide grin stretching across his face.

"She was a neighbour of mine when I was still living with Mom," Elijah explained. "She had the biggest crush on Ken, but was really shy. She would always cling to me whenever he was around. I knew that Ken liked her, too, so one day when we were all in the same room together, I pretended I needed to use the washroom and left them alone, When I returned a few minutes later, they were sitting on the couch and talking and laughing like they had been doing it for years."

"Two years after that we were officially a couple," Kenneth said proudly.

"Congratulations," Lucas said.

"Thanks," Kenneth nodded. "What about you, anyone special in your life?"

Lucas frowned sadly.

"Once, a couple of years ago. But it didn't work out. He moved away. It's not easy being as well known as I am and my dad is. Some people just aren't comfortable with all the attention we receive."

"I'm sorry to hear that," Kenneth said. "But I'm sure you'll find the right person eventually."

"I'm hoping that I already have," Lucas said, with a sideways glance to Elijah and a hopeful grin.

"What, me?" Elijah asked, sputtering into his drink as he caught Lucas staring at him.

"I don't know how often I would watch you as you

floated in the maturation chamber. Even as frail and sick as you were, I knew you were also beautiful. I couldn't keep my eyes off of you. My dad said I was like a lovesick puppy. And maybe I was."

"I thought there was a reason you were waving your tail around at me this morning," Elijah said, with a wide grin.

This time it was Lucas's turn to blush, although thanks to his thick coat of fur, it was hardly noticeable unless someone knew what to look for.

"Maybe it was a little presumptuous of me, though. I'm sorry if I in any way made you feel uncomfortable," he said.

"Oh no, I didn't mind it at all," Elijah assured him. "You really like me, even though you're way older than me?"

Lucas nodded enthusiastically.

"I'm sure I don't have to remind you that we Kindred age differently than you humans do. I may physically be thirty-two-years-old, but as my dad keeps reminding me, developmentally, I'm only about the same age as you and Kenneth are."

"That would make you the oldest seventeen-year-old ever," Kenneth laughed.

"Essentially," Lucas agreed.

"So while I grow older, you'll remain quite young," Elijah said.

"Not any more, though. Once my dad finishes with your treatment, you'll essentially have the same immune system and metabolism as the Kindred, which means you can expect to live a longer life than you naturally would have before if you never had AIDS."

"Cool," Elijah said, actually happy to be hearing this.

All of a sudden Elijah began to feel a little light headed and he had to lean back in the couch or he would have fallen off.

Lucas noticed this right away and called for his father,

who came rushing into the room. He took one look at Elijah and nodded in understanding.

"He's had a bit too much excitement for now. He needs to get a bit more rest," he said.

Elijah was too weak to walk, however. He tried to stand, but fell back down. Lucas asked if he minded if he carried him upstairs and Elijah, with an appreciative grin, shook his head.

Carefully, Lucas lifted him into his arms. Elijah put his arms around Lucas's neck. Doctor Wolff and Kenneth followed them up the stairs to the bedroom where Lucas gently set him down on the bed.

Almost immediately Elijah fell asleep, but not before he felt Lucas lean over him to give him an affectionate kiss on his forehead.

When Elijah awakened for the second time in Doctor Wolff's home he was alone in the room this time and the sun was already high in the sky. This led him to conclude that it was sometime in the afternoon. Whether it was the same day or not, he could not tell, since he had no idea how long he had been asleep. Still fully dressed, he climbed out of bed carefully, feeling a little weak, and walked out of the room and into the hallway.

From downstairs he heard the faint sounds of people talking. Following the voices led him into the living room where he found Lucas and Doctor Wolff sitting across from one another in separate chairs. To his disappointment, though, Kenneth was no where to be seem.

Lucas was the first to notice Elijah and stood up to help him over to the couch, guiding him by the hand with a gentleness that made Elijah smile with gratitude. Despite knowing Lucas for very long, he was quickly becoming very fond of him.

"Did you have a good nap?" Lucas asked when they were seated on the couch.

Elijah nodded appreciatively.

"Yes, thanks. Did Ken go home?"

"He left shortly after you went to sleep. He said he would be by later if you were up to it," Lucas said.

"How long was I asleep?"

"Only for a couple of hours," Lucas replied.

"Care for something to drink, Elijah?" Doctor Wolff asked.

"Yes, please. Some more juice if you don't mind."

With an acknowledging nod, Doctor Wolff left the living room.

When he was gone, Elijah looked fondly at Lucas for a moment, staring deep into his brilliant blue eyes that he was quickly beginning to love so much, before leaning into him and resting his head on the Kindred's warm, soft fur-covered chest. He could feel his strong, steady heartbeat and he felt comforted by it.

"Oh, does this mean you like me too?" Lucas asked with a low-throated chuckle.

"No, your fur just happens to make a really soft pillow to rest my head on," Elijah said sarcastically with a playful grin as he looked up into Lucas's face. "Of course I like you, you silly fox," he almost laughed, snuggling closer into Lucas's chest while casually stroking his fur. "And not just because you saved me either."

"I'm glad," Lucas whispered, running his tongue over Elijah's ear which caused him to shiver with excitement. "I'd hoped you would."

"You make it difficult not to," Elijah replied.

He moaned quietly as Lucas's impossibly long, and extremely flexible tongue again lightly caressed his ear, this time sending tingling shivers running down his spine. He felt another part of him also responding, it also enjoying the attention he was receiving from this beautiful and sensual creature.

Their moment alone, the mood, however, was quickly cut short by Doctor Wolff's return, who frowned when he saw them laying together on the couch. He placed a tray with an empty glass and a full pitcher of juice on the dining room table and looked at Lucas sternly.

"Now you take it easy with him, Lucas, he can't get too excited," he cautioned Lucas.

Lucas gave a little flick of his ears in acknowledgement.

"I know, Dad."

Elijah had to sit up to pour himself some juice and drink it. He certainly didn't want to spill any on Lucas's fur. For some reason, he found himself really thirsty all of a sudden. The first glass he poured wasn't enough to quench his thirst, so he had another, and then a third before he finally felt satiated.

"If you want some more, don't hesitate to ask, Elijah," Doctor Wolff said with a knowing grin. "The treatments will make you fairly thirsty for a few days until you've adapted to the presence of the nanobots in your system."

"Won't my body reject the nanobots?" he asked aloud.

Doctor Wolff shook his head.

"Your immune system was severely compromised because of your AIDS," he began to explain, "so there really wasn't much of one left to begin with. When your immune system eventually re-establishes itself, because the nanobots are programmed to simulate your own DNA, it'll recognize the nanobots as a part of you, allowing them to continue their work unhindered."

Elijah nodded in understanding.

It was at that moment that he then felt the all too familiar hunger pangs stab at his abdomen. This was followed by the rumbling pronouncement by his stomach that it was empty.

Lucas easily heard it, even feeling it through the couch, and snickered slightly.

"Sounds like someone's hungry."

"I guess I haven't eaten a thing since breakfast this morning," Elijah said, blushing with embarrassment.

Doctor Wolff smiled and nodded.

"We've already had lunch, but there is plenty left over," he said. "Lucas, why don't you help Elijah into the kitchen while I get everything ready for him."

FOUR

Rivulets of water washed down Elijah's naked back as he stood under the massaging spray from the shower, letting its warmth seep into his skin and soothe his aching muscles. He ran his hands over his body, noticing the subtle changes that had taken place.

In the five days since Lucas had brought him to Doctor Wolff's house to treat his AIDS, Elijah had begun to fill out considerably. He was still very thin, but he no longer appeared sickly. His strength was returning steadily and he was relying on Lucas for physical support less and less, although he still liked to.

The treatments were not without side-effects, however.

After having lunch, Per invited Elijah up to his lab so that he could inject more modified nanobots into his bloodstream. But soon after receiving the new nanobots, he noticed a growing ache in the muscles in his arms and legs. Per assured him that this was to be expected and that his muscles would most likely ache for the next couple of days. He gave

Elijah some Aspirin to dull the aches.

Lucas had suggested that he take a long, hot shower, which would also help to relieve some of the discomfort. Elijah enthusiastically agreed as he felt the need to get cleaned up anyway.

He had already washed his hair and soaped down his body, and was just standing under the shower, his eyes closed as he soaked in the massaging effects of the water as it rained down on him, when he thought he heard the door to the washroom open and then close.

Opening his eyes and turning his head to the door of the shower, he saw the silhouetted shape of Lucas getting undressed through the frosted glass panel, and then opening the door.

"Got room in there for one more?" Lucas asked, a wide, hopeful grin on his face, tail wagging lazily behind him.

For a brief, shocked moment, Elijah could only stare at him admiringly, his eyes roaming up and down Lucas's naked, furry body. He made no effort to hide his own nudity, though, or his almost instantaneous reaction to Lucas's sudden display of nudity. To do so would have been pointless since Lucas had already seen him naked in the maturation chamber many times before, and again when he had woken up in bed that morning.

Realizing he had been caught staring, Elijah quickly snapped out of his daze, blushing slightly, smiled and hastily stepped aside to allow Lucas to join him in the shower. There was more than enough room to accommodate the two of them.

Since Elijah had already washed, he grabbed the special shampoo that he recognized was specially formulated for Kindred fur, squeezed some of the thick, greenish liquid into his hand and started rubbing it into Lucas's fur. He could scarcely believe it when as soon as he started working the shampoo into a thick, soothing lather that Lucas actually began to purr as though he was a cat, his whole body trembling with intense pleasure.

Ever so slowly Elijah worked his way down until he reached the round, furry cheeks of Lucas's butt and his long, swaying tail. For a moment, he allowed his fingers to linger, squeezing Lucas's butt cheeks gently and feeling the firmness of the muscles under the skin. Lucas, who never made an effort to stop him from touching him in such an intimate manner, instead invited him to continue by pressing back against his hand. Elijah was only too happy to oblige him.

But then, feeling more than a little bit mischievous, Elijah grinned as he ran a lone finger along the crack where the two cheeks of Lucas's butt met, from the base of his tail to the very sensitive spot between his legs. This caused Lucas to gasp suddenly and quiver from the intense pleasure he was experiencing as he opened his legs wider to give Elijah better access.

Although he was thoroughly enjoying himself, Elijah suddenly remembered Doctor Wolff's warnings about not allowing himself to get too excited, and with some reluctance, he stopped playing with Lucas's butt and shifted his attention to his tail which he washed quickly.

Elijah then had Lucas turn around so he could wash his front, and that is when he quickly noticed that the red-tipped end of Lucas's member had partially emerged from within its sheath from all the pleasure Elijah had been giving him.

He smiled up at Lucas knowingly as he then proceeded to wash his shoulders and work his way slowly down to his chest, and then his stomach, until he reached Lucas's waist. He paused here for a moment to admire the impressive results of his ministrations. He purposefully left the rigid member be, however, except to wash around the sensitive, blood-filled organ before continuing down to Lucas's legs and then to his feet.

It took Elijah no more than about ten minutes to complete washing all of Lucas's fur. When he stood up to help Lucas rinse off the soap, he was suddenly drawn into a tight embrace. In his ear he could feel Lucas's heavy breathing.

"That was the most incredible shower anyone has ever given me," Lucas said while trying to catch his breath.

"I hoped you liked it."

"Liked it?" Lucas echoed incredulously, releasing Elijah and holding him at arms length, his whole face beaming with pleasure. "I absolutely loved it!"

"Maybe we can do that again sometime?" Elijah suggested hopefully.

"My sweet Elijah, I can promise you that was the first of many to come," Lucas said as he gently caressed Elijah's cheek. "But next time it's my turn to wash you."

Getting out of the shower, they quickly dried each other off, after which Lucas hurriedly led a suddenly bewildered Elijah by the hand out of the washroom, both of them still naked, to Lucas's bedroom where he had Elijah sit on the edge of the bed. Lucas was clearly excited about something, but Elijah could not quite figure out what. He watched curiously as Lucas reached into the small bedside table drawer and pulled out a long, wire bristled brush. He then sat down beside Elijah, holding the brush out to him with a hopeful expression on his face. It quickly dawned on Elijah why Lucas had suddenly become so eager.

Elijah laughed, accepting the brush from him, as Lucas had effected the perfect puppy-dog look that he had to have known would be impossible for Elijah resist. He was right.

As he proceeded to brush Lucas's long fur, he was fascinated by how quickly loose strands of fur were beginning to accumulate in the bristles, forcing him to remove the mass of fur from the brush several times and throw the clump in the nearby waste basket so that he could continue brushing Lucas down.

"My summer coat is beginning to grow in," Lucas explained with a contented sigh when he caught Elijah's look of amazement as he pulled another clump of fur from the brush. "It'll be a lot shorter than my winter coat soon."

Elijah nodded in understanding.

When Lucas decided he'd had enough, he thanked Elijah and replaced the brush in the bedside table, and then surprised Elijah with a brief, affectionate kiss. He drew back quickly, though, when he felt Elijah stiffen up, and saw the surprise on Elijah's face. He began to fear that he had gone too far with him.

"I'm sorry, maybe I shouldn't have done that," Lucas said, feeling ashamed of himself.

But Elijah smiled back at him, and this time surprising him by pulling him in for a longer, even more passionate kiss. Lucas's surprise didn't last long, however. He returned the kiss with just as much passion, wrapping his arms around Elijah in a loving embrace.

With some reluctance they eventually separated and stared into each other's eyes. Neither of them could any longer ignore the growing passion that enveloped them like a comforting blanket.

I think I'm beginning to fall in love with this boy, Lucas thought. Not that he minded it one bit.

"We should probably get dressed," Lucas suggested breathlessly. "Dad will be getting dinner ready by now, and your friend will probably be arriving again soon."

Elijah nodded in agreement, but he couldn't resist one final kiss with Lucas before he left for his room.

He was lucky that Kenneth had thought to bring him his clothes because he really did not fancy the idea of wearing the same clothes as before. There was nothing especially good in the duffel bag for him to wear, though, he found. A lot of his clothes, although folded neatly, were wrinkled and were in desperate need of ironing. He finally settled on a pair of his favourite tight fitting, slim legged blue jeans and a white polo shirt. Because of the amount of weight he had lost, but thankfully was starting to get back again, he was forced to wear a belt to secure his pants to his waist.

Looking at himself in the mirror on top of the dresser, and satisfied with the way he looked, Elijah smiled and then left his room just as Lucas was also emerging from his own room. He was wearing a white, short-sleeved, loose-fitting tunic and a pair of long shorts which hugged him so close that they accentuated every bump and curve of his body, leaving almost nothing to the imagination.

Wow, he looks so hot! Elijah thought, helplessly captivated by the sight of him.

Lucas chuckled at Elijah's open-mouthed stare, and guided him down the stairs to the dining room where Per had started to set the table. He noticed, with some surprise, that the table was being set for five instead of for four as he expected.

"I received a call from Kenneth while the two of you were busy getting cleaned up," Doctor Woff said, looking up at them. "He will be arriving shortly with his girlfriend, Suzi."

"She's coming, too?" Elijah asked, mildly surprised.

It must have shown on his face because Per smiled at him as he put the last of the cutlery in place.

"Apparently she was excited by the chance to see Lucas. But I suspect that she was mostly worried about you, Elijah."

Elijah nodded in agreement, knowing that Per was right. It would only be natural that she would want to see him since they practically grew up together and there was a real strong friendship between them.

Kenneth arrived at the house only a few short minutes later. And just as Doctor Wolff had said, Suzi was with him. Both were dressed in semi-formal attire, no doubt at the insistence of Kenneth's parents. Elijah smiled knowingly as Kenneth looked distinctly uncomfortable in his black slacks and white dress shirt. He had probably been forced to wear a tie also, but had taken it off in the car.

No sooner did they reach the door when Suzi immediately threw her arms around Elijah, tears freely falling down her cheeks and onto his shirt, getting it all wet. He did not mind, though. He was just as glad to see her as she was to see him. He returned her hug, holding her tightly until she finally released him. There were still tears in her eyes and her cheeks were streaked from the ones that had fallen, but she wore the happiest smile on her face he had ever seen.

"I missed you," she said, in a voice that was barely more than a whisper.

"I missed you, too," Elijah replied.

"Feeling better after your nap, Elijah?" Kenneth asked from behind her.

Elijah looked up at him and nodded, offering him an appreciative smile.

"But hungry," he said.

"Well, let's not wait any longer then," Lucas suggested as he moved out of the doorway to let them all in.

"I can't believe it's really you," Suzi said to Lucas quietly, suddenly noticing him for the first time.

"It was the last time I checked," Lucas snickered.

He extended his hand out to her which she shook happily.

"The girls at school are not going to believe me," she

said.

"Would it help if we took a photo?"

"Really? You wouldn't mind?" she asked, bewildered at Lucas's suggestion.

"Not at all," Lucas laughed as he guided them into the house where Per was waiting patiently by the entrance to the living room.

"Suzi, this is Doctor Wolff, Lucas's father and the one who's looking after Elijah," Kenneth said.

"Doctor, I can't thank you enough for everything you've done for Elijah. When he disappeared so suddenly without saying anything I was afraid I would never see him again," Suzi said, shaking his hand enthusiastically.

"He's a fighter," Per said, "but most of the credit should go to Lucas. If he hadn't found Elijah when he did..." his voice trailed off as he shook his head, not wanting to finish the sentence. They all knew what would have happened if Lucas had not talked him off that bridge.

Suzi looked behind her to Lucas and took particular note of the way Lucas and Elijah were staring at each other, causing her to smile.

Per led them through the living room into the dining room where he invited them all to take a seat. He then disappeared into the kitchen, returning moments later with a large pitcher of juice and several different varieties of soft drinks all of which were on a tray that he placed on the table before disappearing again into the kitchen.

Although Elijah was tempted to reach for one of the bottles of soft drinks, specifically the ginger ale that he had always liked so much, but resisted in favour of the juice which he proceeded to pour into the glass in front of him. He was still in recovery, after all, and thought it was best to drink something healthy to make it easier for his system to heal. A brief glance over at Per who smiled at him and nodded ever so slightly confirmed that he had made the right decision.

Kenneth and Suzi, on the other hand, had no such reservations and did not hesitate to choose their favourite brand of pop.

To Elijah's amazement, though, Lucas also chose to have some of the juice. But then he quickly realized that Lucas had chosen it because of him. He didn't want Elijah to be the only one drinking the juice because he had to. Elijah wanted so desperately right at that moment to lean over and kiss Lucas to thank him for his thoughtfulness, but resisted the urge and instead only smiled. His hand, however, moved to Lucas's lap and give his thigh a gentle squeeze.

The silent exchange between them did not go unnoticed by Suzi, who at first smiled knowingly at them, and then, unable to help herself, let out a little chuckle, drawing their attention to her.

"What?" Elijah asked.

"It's so cute, you guys falling in love like this."

Her sudden declaration surprised everyone in the room, especially Kenneth, who looked clueless as to what was going on. Elijah, on the other hand, was blushing furiously. Had he truly been that obvious? he wondered. She was right though. He knew he was falling in love with Lucas, and it was obvious to him that Lucas's feelings for him were equally as strong.

Lucas was the first one to recover. With a smile, he leaned over and gave Elijah a lingering, and very loving kiss. It shocked Elijah at first, but very quickly he surrendered happily to the kiss.

The sudden sound of Per clearing his throat startled them both and they jumped apart.

"That, I think, can wait until after dinner," he gently admonished them.

"Yes, sir," Lucas said, accepting his father's rebuke.

Per had come into the dining room with a cart containing a veritable feast for them to enjoy. Elijah stared at it in disbelief as Per set each tray of wonderful food on the table. Never before in his life did he see so much food being spread out before him. There was a large roast, potatoes, carrots, and an assortment of other vegetables, a huge bowl of salad, and finally a large bowl containing a very thick, dark gravy. All of it smelled wonderful, causing his mouth to water in anticipation.

When finally the last of the food was on the table, Per sat down in his chair and smiled at them.

"Dig in," he said.

They did not need to be told twice.

After they had finished eating, and after helping Per put the dishes in the dishwasher, they retreated into the living room with some light refreshments, where they could relax and allow the food they ate to settle in their stomachs.

Elijah sat with Lucas on the couch, leaning into him and resting his head on the Kindred's chest while absently playing with his fur. Suzi and Kenneth looked on with amusement from the loveseat opposite them and Per sat in his old chair near the fireplace, a glass of brandy in his hand.

Lighting in the room was subdued, which contributed to and helped create the relaxed atmosphere. It was lit only by two table lamps, sitting on end tables on either side of the couch, and by a number of small wall lamps, two on either side of the door and two on opposite sides of the large window that almost completely spanned the entire length of the room.

By now it was almost completely black outside, with only the faint light from the full moon in the sky providing any source of light. The sounds of crickets singing their song could be heard faintly outside.

"So, you two," Kenneth began, a mischievous smile forming on his face, "when's the wedding?"

"Ken!" Elijah protested, lifting his head up from Lucas's chest and looking at Kenneth sternly.

Lucas just chuckled from under him and Suzi let out a little giggle. Per, meanwhile, just shook his head, but he too was smiling.

"You have to admit, Elijah, the two of you look really cute together," Suzi said.

Elijah put his head back down but looked up at Lucas who was smiling at him. He could see in the Kindred's eyes the fondness he felt for him, and it made his heart sing with joy.

"I love him."

There, he said it, finally openly admitting the feelings for Lucas that had steadily been building within him as he spent more time with him. There was something about the Kindred that was so compelling, and it was more than the physical attraction he felt. Much more.

Elijah reached up to brush the side of Lucas's face with the back of his fingers.

"I do love you," he repeated, quietly.

In response, Lucas pulled Elijah up and gave him the most loving kiss Elijah had ever experienced. Without even saying it, Lucas had just told him he loved him too. He felt that love; in his heart; in his mind; and in his entire being.

"I'm sorry to be the one to have to spoil the mood for you, Elijah, but seeing as how you and Lucas certainly are quickly becoming very close, I think it's appropriate that I ask you how you came to be infected with HIV in the first place," Per said.

"Dad!" Lucas exclaimed, feeling Elijah suddenly tense up.

"No, it's okay, Lucas," Elijah said, trying to calm him down. "Your dad is right to ask since he's only thinking about your welfare."

"I'm glad to see you understand my concerns," Per nodded.

"I was infected by my mom's ex-boyfriend," Elijah said.

"You had sex with him?" Lucas asked incredulously.

"Not by my choice," Elijah replied quietly.

Despite thinking he had finally put the whole episode behind him, tears of pain nevertheless began welling up in his eyes.

"You mean you were raped?" Lucas exclaimed angrily, the fur on the back of his neck beginning to stand up on end.

Elijah could only nod, a number of tears falling down his cheeks.

Lucas quickly realized the pain Elijah was in and held him comfortingly.

"He was at our house one night," Elijah continued to explain, his voice catching, "and I guess he wanted sex from my mom. But for some reason she said no. So later, after my mom had fallen asleep, probably because of how much she had to drink, he came into my room while I was sleeping and he..."

He was unable to finish the sentence as he was suddenly overcome with emotion and began crying as the pain of that night came rushing back to him with a vengeance.

Lucas held him tightly in his arms, in shock and feeling helpless to do anything to help Elijah. All he could do was whisper softly to him that things would be all right, that he would be there for him.

"All this happened about three years ago," Kenneth

continued for Elijah when he saw he was unable to. "Elijah's mother woke up and discovered her ex on top of Elijah, who was screaming in pain. Her ex was arrested, charged, and later convicted of sexual assault of a minor, sexual interference and two counts of aggravated sexual assault, for not disclosing his HIV status."

"The tests came back negative at the hospital," Elijah shakily said with a sniffle. His sobbing had stopped, but tears still fell from his eyes. "We thought I was okay until I started getting sick last year. That's when we learned I was HIV positive. And then a couple of weeks ago my mom learned I was gay and she threw me out."

Per, who had been listening intently to Elijah, had tears of his own in his eyes. All his instincts were urging him to gather up the stricken boy and hold him close in order to protect him as though he were his own son. He slowly left his chair and knelt down before Elijah, putting a comforting hand on his shoulder.

"I'm very sorry to have made you live all that over again, son," he said with as much sincerity as he could muster. "You're very important to Lucas, I can see that. And that makes you a part of this family."

Elijah looked at him, unsure of what he was hearing.

"I can stay here with Lucas then? You won't make me leave?" he asked, voicing the fear that had dwelt in the back of his mind since waking up that morning and discovering that meeting Lucas had not been a dream after all.

Per smiled at him reassuringly.

"Families—true families—do not abandon or reject their own," he said quietly.

Elijah sat up suddenly, practically launching himself in to the arms of Per, who held him in a tight embrace as a father would a son, while Lucas, who could not have been more happy, looked on. Once again tears rolled down Elijah's cheeks, but this time they were tears of joy and relief.

FIVE

The remainder of the evening was spent in casual conversation. Elijah, again in Lucas's comforting arms had managed to get past his earlier discomfort and even began to laugh again when Per relayed to them some of Lucas's more embarrassing situations. Although everyone laughing at Lucas's expense was somewhat uncomfortable for him, even he could not resist a chuckle or two as some of the things he has done, he had to admit, could be considered quite humourous, even though he did not think so at the time.

Eventually, though, Suzi and Kenneth decided it was time for them to go as it was getting quite late and it was a school night. They both thanked Per for a wonderful dinner and Suzi gave both Lucas and Elijah a hug goodbye. She gave Elijah an especially long embrace, telling him that if he ever needed to talk, he only had to call her cell phone.

Soon Suzi and Kenneth were in Kenneth's car, slowly driving down the driveway, through the front gate until they turned onto the street and disappeared from view.

Putting an arm around both Lucas's and Elijah's shoulders, Per led them back into the house and closed the door behind them.

"It's a good idea for the two of you to be getting to bed yourselves," Per suggested. "Tomorrow I want to run some final tests on you, Elijah, to see if the nanobots have done their job."

Nodding in agreement, Elijah and Lucas said good night and then together headed up the stairs.

When they were outside Lucas's room, Elijah gave Lucas a brief kiss before saying good night and heading to his room.

However, he was stopped suddenly when Lucas grabbed a hold of his hand, shook his head and smiled.

"Come join me tonight?" Lucas asked, hopefully.

Elijah looked at him with surprise. He had not been expecting Lucas to ask him to sleep with him.

"Are you sure your dad won't mind us sharing a bed?" he asked.

"After the evening we just had, I think he would be surprised if we didn't," Lucas replied.

Elijah smiled. He had never slept with someone he loved before, and the idea really appealed to him a lot. He nodded and allowed himself, giggling with glee like an excited little school boy, to be pulled into Lucas's room.

Rather than turning on the lights when they entered, however, Lucas led him over to the window where the pale blue light of the full moon fell upon them, casting an almost ethereal glow about them that Elijah thought made Lucas look even more beautiful than before. The light from the moon shown in Lucas's eyes, which glowed brightly.

For a moment they stood in silence, staring into each other's eyes. But then, slowly Lucas began undressing Elijah, who made no effort to stop him. He had no intention or desire to.

Instead he helped him by raising his arms so Lucas could get his shirt off, and stepped out of his pants and underwear when they fell to his ankles. He now stood before Lucas in all his glory, completely naked, again, as Lucas eyed him up and down appreciatively, but paying special attention to his midsection.

Elijah quickly felt that all too familiar tingling sensation between his legs as his body began responding to Lucas's lustful gaze.

This, of course, did not go unnoticed by Lucas who looked up into Elijah's face with a mischievous grin. Before Elijah knew what was happening, Lucas leaned forward, extending his tongue to wrap it around his rapidly growing manhood as he took it all at once into his mouth, as though inhaling it. The suddenness of his attack caused Elijah to moan from such intense pleasure as he had never experienced before in his young life. Certainly never like this with a Kindred doing things that no human was capable of doing.

His knees began to buckle under the relentless assault on his senses. Lucas felt this and led him over to the bed where he gently lay him down all the while continuing to drive Elijah insane with pleasure with his hot, undulating tongue.

In almost no time at all Elijah was approaching the limits of his rapidly diminishing endurance. He could feel the inevitable explosion quickly building to a crescendo within him and knew he would not be able to hold out much longer under the onslaught of Lucas's tongue, no matter how much he wanted to try to hold on just a bit longer.

At last he was no longer able to hold back and with a loud, strangled cry, he exploded his essence and his love hard into Lucas's waiting mouth which continued to work him until the last remaining drop had been greedily devoured.

Elijah could only lie there on the bed, spent and utterly

exhausted, as he soaked in the pleasurable aftershocks of one of the most intense climaxes he had ever experienced. No other could have made him feel as good as he did now, except for the one he loved.

Lucas climbed up Elijah's body, straddling his waist and leaning forward to nuzzle Elijah's nose affectionately, with his.

Elijah, grabbed the side of Lucas's head in his hands, and pulled him in for a deep, passionate kiss. Lucas didn't complain when Elijah then moved a hand deftly down his back to his butt and his wildly swaying tail. Now it was Lucas's turn to moan with pleasure when he felt Elijah's fingers push their way under his shorts and begin to gently massage the cheeks of his butt. Pretty soon, Elijah's other hand joined the first and together began to push Lucas's shorts down past his hips, exposing his butt to the air and giving Elijah the freedom he needed.

Lucas's eyes opened wide with pleasure and he moaned into Elijah's mouth when he suddenly felt a probing digit massage around the most intimate part of him, and even press into him slightly. He raised his head and looked into Elijah's eyes, seeing the love he had for him in them.

"No one has ever touched me the way you are touching me now," he said breathlessly, his eyes half closed with pleasure.

"Do you want me to stop?" Elijah asked.

"No," Lucas said, encouraging him to continue by pressing back on him. "Not ever. It feels so good!"

Elijah chuckled and pressed on, literally, as once again he devouring Lucas's lips in a passion hungry kiss, their tongues entwining rapidly. He could feel Lucas pressing into him, his growing hardness rubbing against his bare stomach, which was beginning to get slippery from Lucas's excitement.

Before long, Lucas's thrusting became even more urgent

as his passion grew, until with one final push, Elijah's finger deep within him, he moaned loudly and Elijah could feel Lucas's explosion splash across his stomach and chest. It never seemed to end, and felt as though the bed would be soaked from their combined love.

End it did, though, and when it did, Lucas collapsed on top of Elijah, his breaths coming in deep gasps. Elijah held onto Lucas, whose fur was matted with sweat, and patiently waiting while Lucas recovered and attempted to catch his breath.

"I never knew," Lucas said breathlessly, "that it could feel so good."

"It can if done with the person you love," Elijah said quietly. "Or so I've heard."

Lucas lifted himself up on slightly unsteady hands, looking down at Elijah with surprise.

"You've never done that before?" he asked.

"Not with any one that I loved," Elijah said, referring to the time he had been forced to have sex with his mother's ex-boyfriend. "I didn't want to do it until I knew it was with someone that I cared a lot for; who I loved."

"I'm glad it was with me," Lucas said.

"Of course," Elijah continued, smiling suggestively. "I think I prefer it the other way around."

"So do I. But I know I want to do that again."

Suddenly, Elijah was forced to look away as he felt the need to yawn.

"You're tired," Lucas observed. "It was probably too much for your body to handle."

"It's a good thing then that we're in bed already," Elijah said, yawning again, more deeply than before this time.

Lucas rolled off of Elijah, pulling off his shirt and adding it to the pile of discarded clothing by the bed. Within seconds he was lying down beside Elijah, who curled up into him, and they closed their eyes. Neither of them thought to clean themselves up. There would be plenty of time for that in the morning.

"I love you, Elijah," Lucas said quietly, kissing his ear.

"I love you, too," Elijah half mumbled.

With smiles on both of their faces, they were soon soundly asleep.

The day that greeted them when they awoke the next morning was dark, grey and rainy. Thick, dark clouds had rolled in overnight, thick dark clouds rolled along the sky, illuminated now and then by the piercing glare of lightning, bringing pelting rain which struck against the window like so many pebbles thrown against the glass.

The miserableness of the weather raging outside, however, could not dampen Elijah's spirits as he lay curled up contently, and warmly, into Lucas's thick-furred body whose arm was draped over his chest and holding him tightly. Elijah could feel Lucas's breath, slow and steady, against the back of his neck, sending pleasurable shivers running down his spine.

He was so comfortable in Lucas's arms, in fact, that at first he failed to realize that sometime during the night they had kicked the covers off of them onto the floor.

Lucas was the first to move, placing a gentle kiss behind Elijah's ear which made him giggle as Lucas's fine whiskers ticked him.

"I wish I could lie here like this forever with you, but unfortunately something else is demanding my attention right now," Lucas said quietly.

Elijah chuckled and turned over to look into Lucas's face.

"Me, too," he said.

With a flurry the two of them scrambled out of bed and crept silently out of the room, down the hall and into the washroom, closing the door quietly behind them.

It was within the closed confines of the washroom, while they were taking care of their business, that Elijah, wrinkling his nose, detected the unmistakable pungent aroma of the previous night's activities that clung to them.

"I think we both could do with a shower," he said, blushing slightly.

Lucas nodded in agreement.

"It smells of our love, and I quite like it," he said with a wry grin. "But I don't think my dad would share that opinion."

"Probably not," Elijah laughed.

Lucas started the shower, checking the temperature of the water before climbing in with Elijah.

They took turns washing each other, rubbing the soap thoroughly over each other and rinsing off. But unlike the first shower they shared together, which had been long and leisurely, and extremely pleasant, this shower was strictly to get cleaned. They both knew Per needed to run some tests on Elijah later to see how his recovery was progressing, and did not want to do anything to jeopardize those results, no matter how tempted they might have been.

They dried themselves off and then went into their separate bedrooms, meeting out in the hallway when they were dressed and together headed down the stairs to the kitchen where Per was already preparing them breakfast. Although he never said anything, both of them suspected he knew what they had been up to that night.

Breakfast was a simple one that morning, consisting of toasted waffles with jam, and orange juice to drink, which they finished in relative silence. Once they had finished, however, Per had Elijah and Lucas follow him back up to his lab.

As before, Elijah was instructed to lie down on the table in the centre of the room. Immediately upon doing so, the table's computer activated and a three-dimensional image of his internal workings and skeleton appeared about a meter above him.

He watched it with fascination as Per approached the table, carrying a pad which he studied intently. The display shifted and magnified specific areas of his body as Per manipulated the controls on his pad. Splotches of blue began appearing wherever Per focused his attention, raising Elijah's curiosity.

"What are those?" Elijah asked, causing Per to look up from his pad to where Elijah was pointing at the image above him.

Per smiled.

"Those are where the nanobots are concentrated most," he said.

The image zoomed in even closer and now Elijah was able to make out the thousands of little robots that were in his bloodstream. Then something remarkable caught his attention, something he was not expecting.

"They're replicating!" he said as the image zoomed back out, showing once again his whole body.

"The nanobots use the raw material of the virus they destroy to help create copies of themselves," Per nodded. "My nanobots are actually part organic, so they derive most of their energy from the organic waste. But because they are also part technological the virus is not able to infect the nanobots and why the nanobots can so easily kill the virus without damaging the surrounding tissues. Once the nanobots have replicated themselves, the new nanobots seek out other sources of the virus."

"But won't they eventually multiply out of control?" Elijah asked with some concern.

"No, the nanobots can only remain operational for a few hours before the biological component dies. The remaining nanobots then reabsorb the dead ones to give them the energy and material necessary to continue their work."

"So why does it sometimes ache then? Is it because of what the nanobots are doing"

Per put down the pad and looked at Elijah carefully.

"Are you in any discomfort now?" he asked.

"A little," Elijah answered hesitantly, "I sometimes feel a dull ache in my stomach."

"Are you sure that's not just indigestion from all those waffles you ate?" Lucas asked

Per shot him a reproving look while picking up the pad again. He tapped a few commands into it and the image above Elijah suddenly shifted until they could see only a close up of his abdomen. There were high concentrations of nanobots there Elijah noted, cringing slightly as he felt another twinge.

"There is some slight inflammation in your upper colon," Per said as he studied the readings on his pad. "But that should disappear rather quickly as the nanobots repair the damage. In the mean time you should take some Aspirin as it will help control the inflammation and the pain."

"Thanks, Doc," Elijah said, smiling gratefully at him.

Per instructed Elijah to then hop off the table. When he did the three-dimensional image of himself promptly vanished as the computer shut down.

"The nanobots appear to have your HIV infection well under control. The next step in your treatment will be to reprogram your natural immune system to resist any lingering infection as well as any future infection that might occur. Essentially what will happen is you will have an immune system that is similar to Kindred's," Per said with a satisfied grin.

"But I'd still be human, right?" Elijah asked.

"No other changes to your physiology will occur," Per nodded. But then added, "unless you want it to."

Something in Per's voice caused Elijah to pause. He was not sure of it, but he thought there was a hint of wishful thinking on Per's part.

Would he really want me to become a Kindred like Lucas? he asked himself.

He had to admit, the idea did hold some appeal to him. He had often wondered while watching the Kindred students at school interacting with humans, what it would be like to be one of them. They appeared to be so sensual and more tactile than humans, who were far more reserved in their interactions with others, at least in private. But he could only imagine, because if his mother had ever found out that he had shown an interest in any Kindred, even as an acquaintance, she would have ripped his hide from his bones for sure.

All of a sudden his eyes opened wide with alarm.

School!

"Doc, what about school?" Elijah asked urgently.

Per looked at him and nodded.

"I had already informed your school that you were staying with us because of your illness. However, if you are feeling up to it, I do not see why not you cannot go back," he said.

"I think I'm well enough now that I really need to," Elijah said.

"There's still time enough for you to make it before classes start for the day," Per said, looking at his watch. "I will drive you there. Do you have everything you need?"

Elijah nodded.

"Kenneth brought me all my school supplies that I had left at his house. The rest is still in my locker at school."

"I'll come with you, but follow you on my own," Lucas said.

"You're not coming in the car?" Elijah asked, shooting Lucas a quizzical glance.

Lucas laughed and shook his head.

"I prefer to run."

Elijah smiled, looking down at Lucas's lithe legs and quickly understanding why running would be his preferred means of travel.

It took him only a few minutes to freshen up quickly in the washroom, gather up his books and supplies from the duffel bag and meet Per outside where Lucas was waiting with him. Elijah saw that except for his shorts, Lucas wore no clothing, not even a pair of shoes.

"There's nothing like a good run like nature intended," Lucas said, catching Elijah staring at him.

"You're still wearing your shorts though," Elijah playfully pointed out to him.

"Remind me to complain to the government about their silly public nudity laws," Lucas said with a slight frown.

Elijah laughed as he then gave Lucas a hug and a short, but passionate, kiss, before climbing into the car.

SIX

Students had already begun gathering out on the front lawn, conversing amongst themselves in those little groups that high school students tended to form, when Elijah and Per arrived at the school only a few short minutes after leaving the house.

Elijah had lost sight of Lucas a few blocks back, but figured he would catch up to them shortly. As they pulled into the parking lot, though, he had to laugh when he saw Lucas standing up against the school wall, looking as leisurely as ever. Somehow he had managed to get to the school before they did, and he did not even look like he had broken into a sweat getting there. He wasn't even panting slightly.

When they exited the car, Per threw a shirt to Lucas as he met them in the parking lot.

"Put that on," Per said to Lucas. "They won't let you inside without it."

Lucas rolled his eyes at his father, but did as he was told.

"Hey, Elijah!" a voice called out, which Elijah quickly recognized as belonging to Kenneth. He turned just as they strolled up to them. "It's nice to see you back, buddy."

"It's good to be back," Elijah answered with a smile.

"I'm glad you made it," Suzi said, giving Elijah a warm hug.

"Thanks."

"We need to get inside to the office to make sure everything is set for you to return, Elijah," Per said.

"Right," Elijah nodded. "I'll see you in class?" he asked Kenneth.

"Of course," his friend answered before he and Suzi walked off so he could walk her to her first period class.

Together, Elijah, Lucas and Per walked to the front doors of the school, ignoring the many surprised glances they received, and whispered voices they heard by the students who had seen their arrival.

It was a little unnerving at first to Elijah, who was not used to the sudden attention they were receiving. But Lucas took a hold of his hand in his, and squeezed it encouragingly. Elijah looked up at him and smiled as they entered the school.

The receptionist at the main office was surprised to see them, to say the least. It wasn't often that a high school, or any public school for that matter, received a visit from such distinguished individuals as Per and his son. In fact, it was very rare. The receptionist was a young man, not much older than Elijah, he guessed, with long, brown hair that was tied neatly at the back in a pony tail and deep brown eyes behind a pair of thick, black-rimmed glasses.

"We're here to speak with Mrs. Bristow," Per said with a friendly smile.

"Of-of course, Doctor Wolff," the shocked receptionist

answered.

He hurried from the counter to an office behind him, knocking on the door gently before going inside. Seconds later he re-emerged with a professionally dressed woman in her mid to late fifties. She wore her black hair, which was greying slightly at the temples, in a tight bun. Of course Elijah recognized her immediately, having seen her before in the hallways sometimes and during assembly. She was the school's Principal, and had been for many years. She always struck Elijah as a very dedicated woman, but also very approachable as well.

Kelley Bristow approached them with a wide, beaming smile when she saw them, and extended her hand to Per to shake, which he accepted.

"Doctor Wolff, this is indeed a great honour," she said.

"Not at all," Per said humbly, waving his hand dismissively. "I'm just here to see that this lad gets to school safely. He's been away sick for some time."

"How are you doing, Elijah?" she asked, looking at him.

"I'm fine now, thanks, ma'am," he replied shyly, surprised that she recognized him.

"And you must be Lucas, Doctor Wolff's son that I've heard so much about," she said shaking Lucas's hand.

"I am," Lucas replied, his ears giving a little flick of acknowledgement.

"Won't the three of you please come into my office where we can talk?" she asked.

They followed her into her office where she directed them to take a seat. The smile on her face disappeared when she sat down as she regarded them carefully.

"It is certainly unusual for a non-custodial adult to be coming to the school with a student. Since your absence from school on Monday, Elijah, we contacted your mother."

Elijah cringed at the mention of his mother, but he remained silent.

"She indicated to us that you had moved out to seek special treatment for your illness," Kelley continued.

"That's a lie!" Elijah exclaimed indignantly, jumping out of his seat.

"Please, Mr. Saunders, control yourself," she admonished him and waited until he had reluctantly sat back down.

She did, however, catch the subtle movement as Lucas, sitting beside Elijah, held his hand for support.

"Sorry," Elijah said. "It's just that I didn't move out. She kicked me out when she learned I was gay."

Kelley gasped in shock, her hand going to her mouth. Homophobia was certainly not unknown to her, but she rarely encountered it, especially not between family members.

"That's just awful," she said quietly. "Where are you staying now?"

"I was staying with a friend before, but now I'm staying with Doctor Wolff," Elijah said, "and my boyfriend," he quickly added while looking at Lucas.

Lucas smiled and nodded as he lovingly squeezed Elijah's hand.

Kelley's smile returned as she looked at them.

"Congratulations you two. When did this happen?"

"Very recently, and very quickly," Per said with a sigh. "Who can keep up with kids these days?"

This caused Kelley to laugh, and even Elijah and Lucas couldn't resist a little chuckle themselves.

"I would hardly call your son a kid, Doctor Wolff," Kelley said. "He's what, in his thirties now? Aren't you concerned about the age difference?"

"Thirty-two this past November," Lucas said.

"But as you well know, Kindred aging is different compared to humans. Lucas was six-years-old when he became a Kindred. Developmentally he's now about the same age as Elijah is."

"Of course," Kelley nodded.

"But getting back to Elijah, when Lucas found him six nights ago, Elijah was hours, if not days, away from death because of how far along his disease had progressed," Per said.

"I had AIDS, Mrs. Bristow," Elijah explained when he saw her shocked expression at what Per had just revealed to her. "I wasn't just HIV positive, but I had full-blown AIDS."

Kelley had to hold herself steady in her chair as she regarded Elijah with horror. But then something he said caught her attention.

"Wait a minute, did you just say you had AIDS, as in the past tense?"

Elijah smiled and nodded.

"I've been treating him for these past few days with a modified treatment I devised a long time ago when I was looking for a cure for Lucas's leukemia," Per explained. "Elijah spent two days in a maturation chamber and then an additional four days of recovery at my residence with my son."

"You've found a cure for AIDS, Doctor?" Kelley asked, completely astounded.

"The cure for all sexually transmitted diseases has been available for a while now, Mrs. Bristow. The government simply refuses to fund the treatment so that it can be made available to all because they fear it would cause more people to want to become Kindred," Per said, shaking his head.

"Elijah will still need time in the maturation chamber to complete the treatment, but he's well enough now that he can return to school," Lucas added.

"I know I have quite a few days to make up for, but I'm willing to do whatever it takes to graduate with the rest of my class."

"I'm sure you will, Elijah," Kelley said, with a gentle smile. But then she frowned.. "The problem is, the law requires us to get a note from a parent or guardian stating the reason for any absence. It must be in the office within forty-eight hours of the time a student returns to school or that absence will be unexcused. This would negatively affect your overall grade, Elijah, and could potentially force you to repeat the year."

She paused and looked at Per.

"Although you are currently caring for Elijah's welfare, you cannot legally be considered his guardian. So I'm afraid if Elijah is to have his absence excused, a note will need to be given to us by his mother."

Per's eyes narrowed noticeably. It was clear he was not liking what he was hearing.

"That is highly unlikely to happen given his mother's wish to have nothing further to do with him," he said.

"Unfortunately the law does not make for any allowances in these types of situations."

"Could the school board not issue a waiver in this case due to Elijah's extreme circumstances?" Lucas asked hopefully.

"Such a waiver would have to be supported by medical documentation detailing Elijah's treatment which would then serve as a valid explanation for his absence," Kelley acknowledged with a nod.

"You will have that waiver, then, by the end of the day," Per promised.

"In that case, I will issue you with an admit slip before you return to your classes, Elijah," she said as she stood from her chair, followed quickly by Elijah, Lucas and Per.

"Thanks, Mrs. Bristow," Elijah said, genuinely grateful.

"You will still need to complete the work you missed, I'm sure you know," she cautioned him.

Elijah nodded in understanding.

Kelley walked them out of the office and had the receptionist they had met earlier complete an admit slip for Elijah. She then shook both Per's and Lucas's hands before returning to her office.

"Would you like me to walk to you to class?" Lucas offered when the receptionist returned with Elijah's slip.

Elijah smiled happily.

"I would like that."

"I will return home immediately then," Per said. "There are some phone calls I need to make."

"Thank you for everything, Doc," Elijah said.

Per smiled at him warmly.

"You just do your best and we'll see you when you get back."

Per then turned and headed back down the hallway to the doors that led to the parking lot outside.

Putting his arm around Elijah's shoulders, Lucas smiled and started with him to Elijah's first class of the day.

A collective gasp of surprise and shock rang out in the classroom when Elijah walked in with Lucas. Heads turned and jaws dropped, including the teacher's, Mr. Thomas Avery, who was seated at his desk waiting for the last of his students to trickle in.

Elijah couldn't tell if they were surprised to see him, after being away for so long, or Lucas, or both. It was likely the latter he decided. Like outside, though, he ignored the looks and allowed himself to be guided lovingly by Lucas to his desk.

Again he heard his classmates' startlement when Lucas leaned down to plant a brief kiss on his lips before leaving the classroom, his tail swaying provocatively behind him for Elijah as he then turned down the hallway.

Elijah smiled and shook his head at the Kindred's antics.

The sound of someone clearing their throat caught his attention and he looked over to see his grade 12 math teacher, Thomas Avery, beckoning him to his desk.

All eyes were still upon him when he got up from his seat again to join his teacher at his desk.

"Mr. Saunders, it's good of you to join us again. I must say you're looking much better than the last time I saw you," Thomas said in a quiet voice so only Elijah could hear.

"Thanks, I had some problems before, but I'm getting better now."

"Have you been given an admit slip from the office?"

Elijah handed him the slip he had received from the receptionist.

Thomas looked at it and nodded, and then made a few notations in his attendance book.

"Come see me after class so that I can give you the work you missed."

"I'll do that, thanks, Mr. Avery," Elijah nodded.

As he returned to his seat, one of the Kindred in his class, a lioness with gold-coloured fur and the hair on her head so long she almost looked like she had a mane, leaned over to him.

"I didn't think you liked Kindred," she whispered, cautiously.

He looked at her with startlement. Had he been so standoffish with the Kindred at his school that they believed he hated them?

"No, I like Kindred just fine," Elijah whispered back. "It's my mom who hates Kindred. I'm sorry that I gave the impression that I hated you. I don't."

She seemed to accept his answer, and even smiled at him.

"Was that really Lucas Wolff who gave you that kiss?" she asked.

He smiled back with an almost dream-like expression on his face.

"He's my boyfriend."

"No way!" she exclaimed, more loudly than she had intended, causing her to fold her ears back in embarrassment as Thomas glared at her from his desk, though her tail flicked with excitement behind her. "When did you two meet?" she asked in a whispered voice when Thomas had returned his attention to his notes.

"A few days ago on the bridge over the river."

"What on Earth were you doing there? she asked, looking at him with a perplexed expression.

Before Elijah could answer though, Thomas stood from his desk to stand at the front of the class, clearing his throat to get everyone's attention.

"Before we begin, I'd like everyone to welcome Elijah back with us. As most of you know he has been sick for some time, so I'm sure we're all glad to see that he's doing much better now."

One of Elijah's classmates, a boy with long, dark, wavy hair, sitting one row in front of him and to his left, raised his hand.

"Yes, Scott?" Thomas said.

"Sir, everyone knows that Elijah has AIDS. But people don't just get better from it," he said.

"It's not for me to discuss with anyone a student's medical history. If Elijah is willing to discuss it with you, you can ask him after class."

Another classmate, a girl with blond curly hair raised her hand also.

"Yes, Sam?" Thomas said, with an impatient sigh.

"Was that actually Lucas Wolff we saw just now?" she asked.

Thomas looked at Elijah, who wanted to sink into his seat. He was not used to this attention, and now he knew what Lucas had meant. He was not about to let that get in the way of what he and Lucas shared, however. Steeling himself he stood up from his seat instead and turned to Sam.

"Yes, that was Lucas Wolff, and he's my boyfriend," he said.

His proclamation caused more gasps from mostly the girls in the room, but also from one or two of the boys as well.

"Alright, people, settle down," Thomas instructed over the chorus of excited conversations that erupted suddenly. He motioned for Elijah to sit back down.

When all conversation had ceased and the classroom was once again silent, except for the gentle humming of the fluorescent lighting in the ceiling.

"Please open your algebra textbooks to the chapter on Linear Equations and Inequalities, and let us review what we've learned."

SEVEN

During the remainder of the school day, Elijah was enthusiastically welcomed back by the rest of his other classmates, even those he didn't recognize, and especially from the Kindred. He felt bad that he had treated them so dismissively in the past and promised himself he would make it up to them somehow.

He had no illusions that part of his new-found popularity had to do with the fact that he had been seen with Lucas by so many when he first arrived that morning. It was all a bit disconcerting, but he tolerated it. Eventually the novelty of it would wear off, he was sure.

During his lunch period, which he chose to spend outside, under a tree, and away from most of the other students, he was approached by the same Kindred girl who had spoken to him in class. As try as he might, though, and to his displeasure, he could not recall her name.

"Mind if I join you, Elijah?" she asked sweetly, her long, thin tail flicking hopefully.

Elijah nodded his assent and moved his backpack so she could sit down next to him.

"I'm sorry, it's a little embarrassing, but I don't even know your name," he said. He could feel his face beginning to flush slightly.

"It's Kiku, Kiku Akiyama."

"Japanese?" he asked.

"My family was originally from Japan, yes," she said, her ears flicking with surprise that he recognized her nationality, even though as a Kindred she was part lion and part human, and in no way resembled her mother, who was human. Her father was a Kindred. "I wanted to apologize for my rudeness to you in class today."

"It's me who should be apologizing. We've spent a year together in the same class and I never once tried to get to know you, to get to know any of the Kindred," Elijah said, looking down at the ground.

"Was your mother really that hateful toward Kindred?"

Elijah nodded slowly, still not looking at her.

"Ever since my dad left to be with one—a gorilla—she's hated you and all Kindred. She blames you for the breakup of her marriage."

"Well that's stupid," Kiku said, her tail flicking in agitation. "Maybe it was her and not the gorilla that caused her marriage to fall apart."

"That's what I think too. My dad has never spoken of it, but I'm sure he knew that they had drifted too far apart to save their marriage. It was by pure coincidence that he met his Kindred boyfriend."

Kiku's ears pricked up in surprise and her eyes opened wide, as did her mouth.

"You mean your dad is also gay?" she asked.

"Well, bi, I think," he said, looking at her and smiling sheepishly.

"I bet she didn't take that well, knowing that he'd chosen a male to be with instead of her."

"You could say that. She hates gays even more than she hates Kindred. Which is why she kicked me out when she found out I was gay."

"So all this time you've been away—"

"I've been homeless, yes," he finished for her. "But not any more."

"No, because you're with Lucas now."

A wide grin stretched across Elijah's face.

"I'd love to meet him," she said quietly.

Elijah barked out a laugh, startling her.

"You and half the school, I'm sure."

Just then a shadow fell upon them, blocking out the afternoon sunlight. Elijah looked up and his smile grew wider still. For there was Lucas standing over them.

"I thought I'd catch you out here on your lunch," Lucas said.

Elijah scrambled to his feet and wrapped his arms around Lucas, planting a lingering kiss on his lips.

"I thought you were with Doc," Elijah said.

"I was, but dad had to go to a meeting with the school board and suggested I spend some time with you. How could I resist?"

Suddenly remembering Kiku, Elijah let go of Lucas.

"This is Kiku, she's in my first period math class."

"It's a pleasure to meet you, Kiku," Lucas said, extending his hand to her.

She shook it gleefull, and probably a little more enthusiastically than she had planned.

Lucas took it all in stride, however, and chuckled when she suddenly let go of his hand, her ears dipping noticeably in embarrassment.

"I'm so sorry, Lucas, you must think me a fool," she said, averting her gaze.

"Not at all, Kiku," he said with a disarming smile. "Believe it or not, I'm quite used to it."

"So, you really are boyfriends?" she asked.

"What can I say, there's no one I'd rather be with more than Elijah."

"That's his way of saying yes," Elijah said, rolling his eyes at Lucas.

"That's so cool."

"Actually, my dad sent me here for another reason also. Shortly after leaving this morning, my dad had what you might call an epiphany. He's asked me to make a presentation to the school this afternoon, and Mrs. Bristow was all for it, apparently, when my dad talked to her about it over the phone."

"About what?" Elijah asked.

"Something that's dear to both our hearts. The eradication of STDs."

Elijah nodded in understanding.

"He hopes to circumvent the government, doesn't he? If they won't fund his research, or even acknowledge it then he'll go directly to the people to try and force their hand."

"That's it exactly," Lucas said, impressed that Elijah was so easily able to deduce his dad's intentions. Is he reading my mind or something? he thought. Aloud he said, "I have to go check in with the office, but I wanted to see you first."

"Lunch period is almost over anyway so we'll walk you there," Elijah decided. He looked at Kiku who nodded her head in enthusiastic agreement.

"Why does your dad all of a sudden have an interest in STDs, Lucas?" Kiku asked as they started back toward the school entrance.

"Probably mostly because of me," Elijah said.

"You're right," Lucas nodded.

"I don't understand, what does it have to do with you, though, Elijah?"

"Well, you know about my AIDS right?"

"Yes," she said slowly.

"This morning you asked me why I was on the bridge. Well, because I knew I was dying, I was there to kill myself."

She looked at him in shock, stopping suddenly, her tail swaying, showing her distress.

"It's true," Lucas said. "If I hadn't found him when I did, he would either have been in the water below, or slumped over, too weak to move. My dad said he only had a day, maybe less before his AIDS would have taken his life."

"I didn't want to go out that way. I wanted it to be on my own terms," Elijah continued.

"But you look fine to me now. Granted you're a little on the thin side, but you don't look sick or anything."

"That's because my dad has been treating him with a modified regimen, similar to the one he used on me to cure my leukemia when I was little," Lucas said.

"So wait, you don't have AIDS any more?" she asked, astonished by what she was hearing.

"Nope, now I've got these little nanobots inside me killing the virus."

"I'm so happy for you!" she said, suddenly throwing her arms around Elijah, surprising him. She sensed this right away and let him go. "Sorry," she said, her ears dipping again in embarrassment.

"Don't be," Elijah laughed. "I had the same reaction with Lucas when he told me."

"Well, maybe not quite the same," Lucas said with a snicker.

Elijah could feel his face growing warm and knew he was blushing furiously.

I love that blush! Lucas thought to himself.

Do you really?

Lucas suddenly stopped with a start, his hand on the door handle, staring at Elijah with a mix of wonder and alarm. The voice was Elijah's, he was certain of it. But it sounded distant, as though he had been speaking from a distance.

"What did you just ask?" he asked a confused-looking Elijah.

"I didn't hear Elijah say anything, Lucas," Kiko said.

"I must have imagined it, then," Lucas concluded, shrugging it off. But still, in the back of his mind, he wondered.

They reached the main office just as the bell sounded, indicating Elijah's lunch period was over. He had to get to his next class, as did Kiku. Before saying goodbye, Elijah gave him a quick, but very tender kiss.

God I love him.

There it was again, the voice. It was clearer this time. He knew it was Elijah's. But how? Already Elijah was walking away from him and heading for the stairs, seemingly oblivious that anything was out of the ordinary.

English Language Studies was normally Elijah's favourite subject, as he loved to read, and loved writing even more. But now it was dragging on at a tortuously slow pace as he waited with growing excitement for the upcoming assembly to be announced on the school's P.A. system. Every time he looked at his watch he was aghast to see that only minutes had past since he last looked at it, even though it felt a lot longer.

When the announcement never came, and the bell eventually sounded to announce the end of the period, he packed up his books and left to go to his next class, Political Science— his least favourite subject.

It was only when Elijah was in the hallway, about to enter the classroom, that the announcement he had been so anxiously waiting for finally came.

"Attention all students and staff. There will be an assembly in the auditorium at two-thirty this afternoon. Fifth period teachers are asked to begin."

Elijah looked at his watch and saw that it was five minutes to two. Plenty of time to get to the auditorium to get a good seat for what he knew was going to be a really interesting assembly, if his teacher let them out early enough.

The rest of his classmates were slowly filing into the classroom. There was a nervous excitement in the air as they discussed quietly amongst themselves this sudden announcement of an assembly. Not one of them had a clue as to what it was going to be about. But of course, there were always the expected idle speculations that teens are notoriously known for. Elijah smiled as he overheard everything from a surprise fire drill to a rally for the school's football team, none of which made any sense to him at all.

Their fifth period teacher was seated at her desk and looking more than just a little unhappy as she stared at the speaker above the door as though willing it to be destroyed. Alycia Bass was known for her strict adherence to routine, and not known for her patience. Any deviation from her carefully planned lessons caused her to become very annoyed. Many students over the years had drawn her ire and were forced to endure some very uncomfortable detentions. Elijah, he was thankful, had never had the honour.

When the last of the students had filed into the room and had taken their seats, Alycia stood from her chair behind her desk and instructed them to not bother opening up their books, but instead to proceed immediately to the auditorium as instructed.

With a relieved smile, thankful that he did not have to endure another one of Alycia's lectures and seemingly endless notes to copy from the projection screen, which she was famous for, he stood back up, slinging his bag over his shoulder and hurried out of the classroom.

He was not the first one to arrive at the auditorium, which featured a raised stage, complete with hanging red curtains that were mostly drawn, from which the school drama class performed many plays and the school band held their concerts for the students and their families. The auditorium also doubled as a lunch room for the students, as well as served as a venue for most of the school's assemblies.

There were many rows of what Elijah considered to be the most uncomfortable chairs he had ever had the pleasure of sitting in. They were mostly metal, with minimal padding on the seat to cushion the butt, and none for the back, and were the type that collapsed so they could easily be stored when not needed.

The seats nearest the stage were largely empty, as there were only a few students in the auditorium. That would quickly change, though, as more students arrived, and indeed he already saw more arriving behind him. He quickly made a beeline for the front row, where he knew Lucas would be able to see him, and sat down in a chair near the centre of the stage before anyone else could claim it.

He was, moments later, joined by Kiku, who had also had the presence of mind to come as quickly as she could so she could get a good seat. She was not at all surprised to see Elijah sitting where he was, given who would soon be addressing the school.

The slow trickle of students filling the auditorium quickly became a massive rush as the rest of the entire school attempted to find a seat in the room. Although the auditorium was quite large, it was quickly becoming very congested. Some students were unable to find a seat at all and were forced to stand at the back wall or along the sides with the teachers.

Elijah could barely hear himself think over the din in the room as hundreds of students engaged in overlapping conversations. But then Kelley Bristow, the school's principal, appeared on stage, standing in front of a microphone which she tapped gently to get everyone's attention. Slowly the conversations tapered off until it was quiet in the auditorium.

"Good afternoon, Fraser Heights!" she said loudly into the microphone, prompting the whole school to pump their fists into the air and recite the school's cheer.

"I would first like to thank all of you for coming to this special assembly this afternoon," she continued. "I'm sure that most of you are probably happy to be getting out of the classroom."

To this, there were happy cheers and some laughter. She smiled.

"But I'm also sure none of you came here to listen to me speak."

To that there were some muted chuckles and more than a few heads nodding in agreement.

"So without further delay, I'd like to introduce you to a very special guest. Most of you, if you were actually paying attention in class, should already know him from your history books, though only a few here have actually met him in person. And there is even one among you who shares a very special bond with him."

Kelley's gaze immediately fell on Elijah in the front row, who was beginning to blush from the attention.

"Please give a very warm Fraser Heights welcome to Mr. Lucas Wolff!"

There was a loud collective gasp from the entire school, including the teachers, as Lucas strolled confidently out onto the stage to stand with Kelley. Once the shock of his appearance had worn off, the entire school leapt to their feet to enthusiastically welcome Lucas to their school with thunderous applause.

EIGHT

To Elijah it seemed the applause would go on forever. Eventually, though, the applause did finally begin to gradually die down as the school eventually retook their seats—those who had been sitting that is.

Lucas looked at them all with a wide, toothless grin, his tail swaying the only indication of any nervousness.

"Thank you, Principal Bristow for that most generous introduction. And thank you Fraser Heights for your very warm and heartfelt welcome. I am deeply honoured to be here with you today.

"It's not very often that I'm asked to speak in front of such a large group of people like this. In fact, I don't think I've had to since my college days."

There was some snickering in the crowd.

"But my father, Doctor Per Wolff, has asked me to address you this afternoon on a very important topic," Lucas continued. "Before I begin, though, I first would like to refresh your memories by taking you back in history."

He was met with a few groans in the crowd, which he easily heard thanks to his excellent hearing. But his smile never wavered.

"About twenty-six years ago our world was plagued by the scourge of terrorists and religious and political extremists of all sorts. To counter this threat, my father was contacted by the World Government to create for them an army of super-soldiers that would be capable of dealing with this threat once and for all. My father's solution was the Kindred. I was only six-years-old then, and terminally ill with leukemia at the time. My father's one stipulation to the World Government before accepting such a task was that he be allowed to make me the first of the Kindred. They reluctantly agreed.

"We are called Kindred because my father believed, as I do, that humanity alone cannot be master of our world. We share this wonderful planet with many amazing creatures that my father considered kindred spirits. He believes that only by embracing all of Mother Nature's wonderful gifts can humanity hope to truly flourish."

Here Lucas paused as he scanned the room. Everyone assembled was hanging on his every word, staring up at him in awe. It was probably the first time any of them had heard the reasoning behind the Kindred's name.

"The Kindred were not just given the appearance of the animals who's DNA we share, but we were also given a heightened immune system. It is this immune system that brings me here today."

Elijah watched from the crowd, impressed by how easily Lucas was able to command the attention of the audience. Half-jokingly, he thought he would make an excellent politician.

Watch it!

The silent, but unmistakeable rebuke startled Elijah and he looked around. But no one was paying attention to him. All eyes were on Lucas. Lucas, on the other hand, Elijah saw, shot him a reproving glance under which he felt properly chastised.

"Several nights ago," Lucas continued, once again looking up and smiling, "as I went for a stroll, as I often do, I came across a young human male. He was clearly distraught and it seemed to me he had almost completely lost the will to live."

Elijah knew Lucas was referring to him, and was relieved that Lucas had omitted the part about him wanting to take his own life.

This time Lucas smiled warmly at him, the love for him shining brightly in his eyes.

"I learned from speaking with him that this young man had AIDS. He was so thin and frail-looking, and weak, that I knew without medical attention there was a good possibility he would not be alive for much longer. I made up my mind then to do the only thing I could think of, which was to bring him to my father."

Lucas paused here to gather himself. He had not expected the retelling of his rescue of Elijah to make him so emotional. He had to fight back tears as he recalled that frightful night, and only continued when he had managed to regain some semblance of control.

"My father confirmed what I had already known, that without treatment he would be dead within a day, if not hours. What he needed, my father determined, was an immediate infusion of modified nanobots to fight off the infection and to allow his own natural immune system to reassert itself, and a genetic resequencing to enhance his immune system so that it would make his system immune to further infection. After five days in the maturation chamber, I'm pleased to say the first part of the treatment has worked. The young man is now free of AIDS and his system shows no signs of the HIV infection anywhere in his system. As incredible as it might seem, my father has cured this young man of AIDS."

A shocked silence greeted Lucas when he finished, a low excited murmur spreading among some of the students.

"Elijah, would you join me up here, please?" Lucas asked.

Lucas's request had momentarily startled Elijah, who froze in his seat. He had not been expecting to be called up on the stage. Ultimately, it was Kiku who gave him the nudge necessary to get him to finally ascend the steps leading to the stage, still in a bewildered daze, until he had joined Lucas by his side.

"Some of you may know Elijah Saunders, either from class or outside of school. Many of you who know him also knew that he had AIDS. It wasn't a secret that he kept from anyone. But now, I am very happy to say, thanks to the efforts of my father, he is now completely clear of the virus that had given him AIDS and almost robbed him of his life. I would encourage everyone to join with me in applauding him the tremendous courage it took to face down this horrible disease, and win!"

Elijah looked lovingly into Lucas's eyes as the entire school leaped to their feet and erupted again in thunderous applause, some of them even cheering, and it grew even louder when Elijah wrapped his arms around Lucas in a tight embrace. He had tears in his eyes, that fell from his cheeks onto Lucas's tunic. But they were happy tears that went with the very happy smile he wore on his face.

"Oh just kiss him already!" Kiku loudly called out,

causing some in attendance to laugh at her outburst. It did not bother her in the slightest.

Shrugging his shoulders, Elijah did just as Kiku suggested, pulling back slightly to give Lucas the most tender, loving kiss he could, much to the amazement of everyone in the crowd.

They reluctantly separated, staring into each other's eyes for a moment before Lucas slowly turned to the microphone where he waited until the applause had died down.

"As you can see, we've grown quite attached to each other," he said.

That produced a round of laughter from everyone in the auditorium. Elijah smiled happily at Lucas. When they got home...

Can't wait!

Elijah's eyes opened wide in shock as he stared at Lucas in disbelief.

"But I did not come here to introduce you to my new boyfriend," Lucas continued, speaking to his audience as though oblivious to Elijah's reaction. "It is my father's wish that not just Elijah, but all of humanity that benefits from this breakthrough, and diseases like AIDS will someday be a thing of the past. To that end he will be talking to the university about funding my father's research, and I am here to announce that as part of that research, he will be looking for volunteers, anyone who has come into close intimate contact with anyone with a sexually transmitted infection, or who may have contracted one themselves."

He slowly scanned the auditorium and saw the shocked reaction of the students and teachers in the room. But in some of their eyes he saw a flicker of hope. He made sure he burned their faces into his memory as he was sure he would be seeing them again soon.

"Your school has already received a rough outline of my father's research, including details of Elijah's treatment, which will be sent to each of your parents to look over. If the University agrees to provide funding for this research, within the next couple of days permission slips will be sent to each of you which will need to be signed by a parent or guardian should any of you wish to participate."

A boy, who Elijah did not recognize unexpectedly stood up from the third row.

"Excuse me, Mr. Wolff, what about students who may be HIV positive, or have another type of infection, but don't wish their parents to know?" he asked.

Lucas smiled reassuringly at the boy.

"As with any study of this nature, the identity of participants is strictly confidential. If any student is hesitant to involve a parent or guardian, they can still participate by having their doctor refer them to my father. The same outline that has been sent to your parents has also been sent to every medical practitioner in the province."

"Why have you not gone to the government with this? It seems that this is something the government would really be interested in," a girl at the back of the auditorium asked.

"The government was approached, but has decided against funding the research." Lucas answered with a frown.

It was not an answer the students, or the teachers for that matter, were expecting. For the government to decide not to fund research that clearly had the potential of greatly improving the lives of its citizens came as quite a shock to them.

A teacher raised his hand, and Elijah instantly recognized it as belonging to Thomas Avery, his grade twelve math teacher.

"Mr. Wolff, forgive me for asking, but my nine-year-old daughter, Melissa, was diagnosed with acute lymphoblastic leukemia two years ago. Even with intensive chemotherapy, though, her condition continues to deteriorate and the doctors feel she may never respond to treatment. I know your study is meant to find ways to eradicate diseases like HIV, but is there anything that can be done for my daughter?"

Elijah could see in his face that he was filled with a desperation that only a parent with a terminally ill child could know. It was not difficult to see that he was in pain having to watch his daughter suffer and know there was nothing he could do, even though every fibre of his being was driving him to do something, anything, to help her. He could almost feel the helplessness of the man. It was a side of him Elijah had never seen before.

"As you know, I suffered from that same form of leukemia when I was a child. The doctors then did not hold much hope of me surviving past my seventh birthday either. My father can help your daughter like he helped me, but it would necessitate an almost complete resequencing of her genes and she would not be the same afterward."

"Please, if anything can be done—"

"Even if that meant she would become Kindred?" Lucas asked seriously, cutting him off in mid sentence.

Thomas did not even hesitate for one second. He nodded his assent.

Lucas smiled at him reassuringly.

"Come see me after the assembly, if you are free, and we can discuss it further."

"Thank you, Mr. Wolff," Thomas said gratefully.

After answering a few more questions, Lucas thanked them for their time and allowed Mrs. Bristow to take over the microphone. When she did, she promptly dismissed the assembly, coincidentally only mere seconds before the bell rang signifying the end of the school day.

Elijah stayed with Lucas as the auditorium slowly emptied. Eventually they were the only ones remaining, except for the janitorial staff who proceeded to fold up all the chairs and rest them against the wall. Grabbing his hand, Elijah led Lucas off the stage and they too left.

It took Elijah only a few minutes to collect his things from his locker, after which they proceeded to the main office where they quickly saw Per was standing with Thomas in the hallway.

Per heard their approach and turned to greet them.

"How was school, Elijah?" he asked, with a warm smile.

"It was school," Elijah replied.

Per smiled knowingly.

"Did you get your assignments that you missed while you were absent?"

Elijah nodded and patted his bag, indicating that he had them with him.

"I was able to get the waiver for you, Elijah, and I'd just given it to the receptionist so you're all set. But then I bumped into Mr. Avery here."

"Hello again, Mr. Avery," Lucas said, offering his hand to him. "I was sorry to hear about your daughter."

Thomas shook Lucas's hand warmly, but firmly.

"I can't thank you enough for giving me the chance to discuss this with you and your father."

"Mr. Avery's daughter has terminal cancer, acute lymphoblastic leukemia," Lucas said, seeing his father's inquisitive look. "He's asked if there's anything that can be done to save her."

Per nodded, his brow crunching up in thought.

"I'm sure my son has informed you that while treating your daughter is possible, it would require some extensive changes to her DNA. She would not be the same afterwards."

"But she would be alive," Thomas said. "My wife and I have been desperate to find something to help our daughter. The doctors say there's no hope for her, though."

Per snorted derisively.

"Doctor's, what do they know?"

Lucas snickered from amusement. It was no secret to him how his father felt about medical doctors. He trusted them about as much as he trusted the weather reports.

"Which hospital is your daughter at?" Per asked, ignoring Lucas's reaction.

"Surrey Memorial Hospital."

"Do you think it would be possible that we could visit her?

"Of course," Thomas said, nodding enthusiastically. "Right now if you'd like. My wife is with our daughter and I was going to see her anyway after finishing here."

Lucas looked at his father hopefully, and smiled when Per nodded his assent.

Thomas's eyes glistened wetly as they filled with hope for the first time in what seemed like ages.

They left the school together, Thomas hurrying to his car in the parking lot. Per had parked his car in a spot reserved for visitors. They climbed in, including Lucas, much to Elijah's surprise.

"Don't you prefer to run?" he asked.

"Don't want to be all sweaty for when we meet the girl," Lucas replied with a smile.

Elijah nodded in understanding. He put a hand gently on Lucas's thigh, giving it a tender squeeze.

"I'm so glad you have such a kind heart. It makes me love you more and more."

Lucas leaned over and lightly teased Elijah's ear with his tongue, causing Elijah to shiver with pleasure.

"And I love you, too," he whispered, "even if you think I'd make a good politician."

Elijah looked at him in shock.

"So that did happen then."

Lucas nodded.

"How-how did you hear what I was thinking?" Elijah stuttered.

"I don't know. But I've noticed it's happened several times now. We'll have to talk to my dad about it when we finish at the hospital."

Elijah nodded in complete agreement. This was just too weird.

NINE

They learned Thomas's daughter's name was Aurora when they met him at the hospital and were invited into his daughter's room.

She was awake, and staring at them with curious interest from the hospital bed that she was sitting up in. The moment she saw Lucas enter the room, though, the curious smile on her face became one that instantly stretched from ear to ear.

Beside her was an older woman, who Elijah guessed was Thomas's wife and the girl's mother. She had been reading to Aurora when she noticed them entering the room with her husband.

"Who's this, Tom?" she asked, closing the book and putting it on the bed.

"Honey, this here is Doctor Per Wolff and his son Lucas. This other young man is a student of mine, Elijah Saunders, and Lucas's boyfriend. Gentlemen, this is my wife, Nelle."

She stood up from the chair she had been sitting in to greet them.

"It's very nice to meet you all," she said, shaking each of their hands. "Although I'm a little confused as to why my husband would bring you here."

Lucas, with his attention focussed on Aurora, walked right to the recently vacated chair and sat down next to the little girl.

She watched him carefully, still smiling. He smiled back at her.

She was bald, Lucas noted, a side-effect of the chemotherapy treatment she was receiving, and she was dressed in a thin, pink-coloured hospital gown with tiny little flowers printed all over it. Attached to her arm was an intravenous line, feeding her the medicine she needed.

"Hello," Lucas said warmly.

"Hello."

"I'm Lucas. What's your name?" he asked.

"Aurora." she said.

"That's a beautiful name."

She smiled proudly. With her free hand, she reached out to touch his fur. He let her.

"It's so soft."

"Thank you," he said, "though it does need a brushing."

"I can do that for you," she said, her eyes opening wide with instant enthusiasm. She looked past him to her mother. "Can I mom?"

Nelle smiled and nodded to her daughter.

From the small pouch that Lucas kept around his waist, he pulled out a small brush which he handed to the girl. Then, as he leaned forward so she could better reach him, she quickly began to brush the fur on his head gently, causing Lucas to purr with pleasure. She giggled happily when she felt the subtle vibrations he was making as he really begin to enjoy the brushing she was giving him.

"So what's all this about, Tom?" Nelle asked, turning back to look at her husband.

"As I said this is Doctor Wolff and his son. They're here because they say they may be able to help our daughter."

Nelle's eyes opened wide with surprise.

"How?" she asked.

"Well, Doctor Wolff, as you know, is the one who created the Kindred. His son was the first one. But also, Lucas had the exact same type of cancer that Aurora has, and Doctor Wolff was able to cure him."

"How," she asked, quietly.

"As I explained to your husband, Mrs. Avery, the disease your daughter has can be cured, but it would require some extensive alterations to her DNA. And she won't be the same when it is complete."

"She would become Kindred, dear." Thomas said.

Nelle's hand flew up to her face as she gasped in shock.

"It might be her only chance," Thomas concluded.

"But to become Kindred..." Nelle said, her voice trailing off as she looked back at her daughter who was happily brushing Lucas's fur, now working on the fur on his arms.

"Mrs. Avery, it's not so bad," Lucas said, looking up at her. "When my dad cured me of leukemia and made me Kindred, I was only six-years-old. My dad even made sure that I was able to pick what I would look like. I chose to be a fox because it was so like one of my favourite cartoon characters on TV."

"Before considering to go through with this procedure, though, I need to know that this is what she wants. That is why I asked your husband to bring us here, so that we could talk to her," Doctor Wolff said.

Elijah could see that she was thinking about it hard, her brow furrowing as she thought it over.

"Aurora has always been fascinated with the Kindred," she said slowly.

She closed her eyes for a moment, and as though coming to a decision finally nodded in agreement.

"I want my baby to live. But you're right, it wouldn't be fair to make this decision for her."

Lucas, easily hearing this quiet conversation, looked at Aurora.

"What's your favourite animal in the whole wide world, Aurora?"

She giggled at the question, thinking it was a silly thing to ask right then when she was brushing his fur.

"That's easy, it's a tiger," she said.

"Have you ever wondered what it would be like to be a tiger?" he asked.

Aurora nodded excitedly.

"Oh yeah, I used to pretend I was a tiger when I played with my cat when I was real little."

"Do you know what a Kindred is, Aurora?"

She rolled her eyes at him.

"Of course, silly. You're Kindred," she said.

Lucas chuckled, and behind him he could also see Elijah smiling.

"And what about the kinds of Kindred there are, do you know them?"

Aurora's tiny nose scrunched up as she began to think.

"There's foxes, wolves, lions, bears, gorillas and—"

"And tigers," Lucas finished for her.

It took her a few moments, but then her eyes opened wide when it suddenly dawned on her what Lucas was suggesting. She looked at her parents who stood with Per and nodded at her.

"I can actually become a tiger?" she asked softly to Lucas.

"If you want to. It would also mean you would no longer have leukemia."

"No more hospitals?" she asked hopefully.

"Not unless you were to see a friend or if you got really hurt."

"Can I, Mom? Can I, Dad?"

"There's just one thing," Lucas cautioned her. "You will need to be asleep for a long time—at least a couple of weeks—because it will hurt while you are changing."

She frowned at this. She didn't like pain. She had experienced too much of it in the last couple of years.

Just then Elijah stepped forward to join Lucas. He put an arm around Lucas's shoulder.

"I've already been in the maturation chamber, Aurora," Elijah said. "I was asleep the whole time I was in there and didn't feel a thing."

"Do you have leukemia too?" she asked with concern.

Elijah smiled at her reassuringly. He could see that she had a very gentle heart, just like Lucas did.

"No, I had AIDS. But Doctor Wolff and Lucas were able to make me all better. And if you let them, they can make you all better too."

"We'll be there the whole time you're in the maturation chamber, sweetie, your dad and I," Nelle promised her.

"Okay," she said, her smile returning. "I want to become a tiger and get better."

"I will return home then to make the necessary preparations," Per said. "Lucas, you will show them how to get to the house?"

"Of course, Dad," Lucas nodded.

"I guess I'd better go have a talk with the doctor to have Aurora checked out of the hospital," Thomas said.

Nelle had just managed to help Aurora off the bed and was leading her to the small washroom opposite the bed to get changed when they heard the sound of angry voices just outside the door in the hallway.

Lucas could clearly tell it was Aurora's father's voice he heard and the voice of another man he did not recognize. He nodded to Nelle to take Aurora into the washroom while he stepped outside the room with Elijah. There they saw Thomas standing in front of the door as if guarding it from the younger man who appeared to be a doctor. Both men's faces were flush with anger.

"What's going on out here?" Lucas demanded, rising to his full, imposing height, which to Elijah was impressive as he gawked up at him. Lucase had to have been seven feet tall, at least.

Both men stared at him in shock. Neither of them had heard him come out into the hallway. The doctor reeled back slightly from Lucas.

"We can hear you two clear into the next room and you're frightening a little girl," Lucas said in a tone of voice that would brook no argument, his tail swaying behind him angrily and his ears folded flat against his skull.

Elijah had never seen Lucas like this before, and was in awe of him. Strangely, though, it did not intimidate him like it did the poor doctor, who was stammering away and trying to find his voice.

"I was just telling Mr. Avery here that his daughter is too sick to be moved. She needs her rest and her treatments need to be continued if there is any chance for her survival."

"But you have already indicated that despite your best efforts, she isn't responding to your treatments. Is that not correct?" Lucas asked leaning down and stepping forward until they were almost nose to nose.

"Y-Yes."

Elijah thought the doctor was actually going to pee his pants. He had to suppress a grin.

"Do you know who I am?" Lucas finally asked.

The doctor nodded slowly.

"You're Doctor Wolff's son, Lucas."

"And his lab assistant, and his former patient," Lucas finished for him."My father has offered to give Mr. Avery's daughter the same treatment he had given me two decades ago. It will save her life."

"Doctor, you know what Doctor Wolff was able to do for Lucas, and what he can do again for Aurora. He's willing to take responsibility for her care, and her parents have already agreed to the procedure. What's more, she has agreed as well," Elijah said, choosing to use a gentler voice.

"But she's just a child. She can't make that kind of decision," the Doctor said, shaking his head. "That procedure will change her. She won't be human any more."

Elijah smiled.

"No, she'll be a tiger, her favourite animal," he said. "Would you really deny her the opportunity to live when the hospital cannot do anything more for her except to try and make her comfortable until she passes away?"

Now who's the politician? Lucas thought, staring back at Elijah with a smile.

Elijah heard the comment, but chose to ignore it. They were even now, he guessed.

Eventually the doctor ceded Elijah's point and nodded in reluctant assent.

"I will sign the paperwork," he said, and then looked back up at Lucas. "But I will need you to sign as well to approve the transfer to your father's care."

Lucas relaxed visibly and returned to his normal height, nodding his agreement.

"Remind me not to get you angry," Elijah said, whispering into his ear. And then, out of a whim, he teased his tongue inside the Kindred's ear.

Lucas shivered all over, smiling appreciatively at Elijah.

My bed or his tonight? Elijah wondered as he noticed the slight movement in Lucas's shorts.

Yours, definitely.

Elijah wasn't even surprised by the response this time. He was getting used to it by now.

They walked back into the room, with the doctor, where Aurora was again sitting on the bed with her mother standing next to her. Aurora was completely dressed now, except for her shirt which she only had one arm in. She couldn't put the other arm in the shirt because of the intravenous line still attached to her.

The doctor quickly moved to Aurora, where he slowly, and carefully removed the intravenous line from her arm. There was no blood, but from a drawer in the table next to the bed, he removed some cotton, some antiseptic wipes, and a fresh bandage which he used to clean and then cover the puncture site. She didn't even wince when he rubbed her wrist gently with the wipes.

That done, Aurora was able to finish putting her shirt on. Elijah thought it must have been her favourite because the front of the shirt had a large picture of a tiger on it.

Not wanting to spend another moment in the hospital, they left for the main lobby where the doctor had Thomas and Lucas sign the appropriate paperwork, and then Thomas led them out to the parking lot and to his car.

Elijah and Lucas sat in the back with Aurora who sat in the middle between them, as they left the hospital. He caught Nelle looking back at them and smiling when she saw Aurora leaning comfortably into Lucas's fur and closing her eyes contentedly.

Lucas's directions were very precise so Thomas had no difficulties finding the house. Both Thomas and his wife appeared very impressed with the estate the house sat on, as they passed the front gate and saw the beautiful gardens and trees that surrounded it.

"My father allows the University's Botany Undergraduates to maintain the grounds here which they can use as experience to gain extra credits towards their degrees," Lucas said, answering both their unanswered question.

Thomas parked the car next to Per's which was already parked in front of the small garage.

Holding Elijah's hand, Lucas then led them all inside the house. From behind them they heard Aurora's tiny giggle.

"Guess she's never seen two guys in love before," Elijah whispered with a smile to Lucas, shrugging his shoulders.

Per was waiting for them inside, and led them into the livingroom where he invited them to take a seat.

"Doctor Wolff, when do you think you will be able to begin the procedure?" Thomas asked, getting right to the point.

"The maturation chamber is filling now, which will take an hour to complete," Per said. "In the mean time, while we're waiting, I thought you all might enjoy some dinner. I'm sure you're all hungry."

It was right at that moment that Elijah's stomach suddenly decided to make its presence known.

"I think that would constitute one vote in favour of dinner," Thomas said.

"Teenagers are always hungry," Nelle added, "just like certain nine-year-old-girls I know."

"No I'm not," Aurora protested, but then her stomach rumbled as well, causing her to blush a deep crimson colour.

"I'd better get the table ready then," Per said, smiling as he stood up once again.

"I'll help," Elijah said.

He started to get up as well, but Per waved him back down.

"No, it's alright, Elijah, I've got this. You keep our guests company with Lucas."

Elijah nodded and settled back down to cuddle with Lucas.

"It's so cute to see the two of you so in love with each other," Nelle said, beaming happily at them.

"It honestly took us both by surprise as well," Lucas nodded.

Dinner was a largely quiet affair, with very little conversation except the occasional question or two from Thomas and Nelle about the procedure to turn their daughter into a Kindred. Aurora listened to her parent's questions intently, as well as the answers given, but understood little of it. It didn't matter to her, though. She was going to become a tiger and no longer have leukemia, and that is all that really mattered to her.

After dinner they rested a bit before Per announced that the chamber was now ready and they headed upstairs to Per's lab where the huge tank was set up in the corner, filled with the nutrient rich greenish fluid that would make Aurora's transition possible.

Per instructed that Aurora would have to be submerged without clothing. That was something Aurora was not expecting and became instantly hesitant.

Lucas approached her and knelt down to the nervous child.

"Hey, it's all right. Both Elijah and I had to do the same thing so that we could get better. Besides, if you wore clothes in there when you change, they could hurt you because you will grow a little."

She raised her head, still nervous about being naked, but caught onto something he said that made her smile.

"Will I be as tall as you?" she asked.

Lucas chuckled lightly.

"Not quite. You'll still have some growing up to do, but you'll be beautiful as a tiger. I know it."

This time she smiled widely and nodded.

To protect her modesty somewhat, she was offered a towel while she undressed. Lucas, Elijah and Per found something of interest to focus their attention on until she was ready.

Per gave Thomas and Nelle one last chance to change their minds about going through with the procedure, for once it started, it could not be stopped, and once it was done it could not be reversed.

Both of them declined.

With a nod of understanding, Per prepared the injection that would put Aurora into a deep sleep.

Thomas caught her as she quickly began to tire, closing her eyes, and soon she was limp in his arms as she fell unconscious.

Per fitted the modified rebreather over her face and

attached the intravenous lines into her arms that would keep her unconscious during the procedure and feed her the nanobots that would make the change happen. Then, with Thomas's help, they lifted the small girl into the tank and slowly, carefully, slipped her into the maturation chamber.

The towel that until now had protected her modesty fell away from her as she sunk deeper into the greenish fluid. Her body, however, instinctively curled itself into a ball, assuming a foetal position, to protect itself.

As Nelle and Thomas looked on through the glass at their sleeping daughter, floating seemingly weightless in the tank, Nell approached the tank and put her hand on the glass by her daughter's head.

"I'll see you soon, baby," she said quietly, a single tear rolling down her cheek.

TEN

Elijah made love to Lucas that night in his bedroom. The drapes had been drawn back, allowing the blue light of the moon to cast an ethereal glow about Lucas as he hovered above Elijah, panting heavily.

Their two bodies were as one, rocking back and forth in perfect sync.

Elijah looked up lovingly into the Kindred's eyes as Lucas thrust deeper into him. His legs were raised and wrapped around Lucas's back, encouraging him, no, needing him, to be as deep inside him as possible.

Never in his life could have imagined it could feel this good to give himself fully to the one person in all the world that he loved with all his heart.

The quiet sounds of desperate moans of pleasure filled the room, growing with intensity and volume as the two lovers rapidly approached their climaxes together.

With one great final thrust, Lucas embedded himself deep within Elijah. Raising his head, he howled as he exploded with such force he almost blacked out.

Beneath him Elijah's eyes opened wide as he found himself suddenly stretched wider and penetrated deeper than ever before. The combination of pain and pleasure triggered his own explosion to burst forth from within him, its pulsing wetness spreading between them.

When it was all over, Lucas collapsed on top of him, still buried deep within him and panting heavily from his exertions. There was a satisfied grin both their faces. Elijah held onto Lucas tightly as they lay basking in the warm afterglow of their lovemaking.

All of a sudden a rap on the door startled them, followed by Per's muted voice out in the hallway.

"Would you two mind keeping it down in there? There are people in this house wanting to sleep without having to listen to you baying at the moon!"

Elijah couldn't resist a giggle.

"Sorry, Dad," Lucas called out.

They could then hear Per's footsteps on the hardwood floor disappearing down the hall.

"I think if we want to do that again we should probably do it in your apartment," Elijah suggested quietly, then quickly added, "And I do want to do it again. Again and again and again!"

"So do I," Lucas said with a slight chuckle.

Slowly, with care so as not to injure Elijah, Lucas disengaged from him and rolled over onto his back.

Elijah turned onto his side, facing Lucas, and cuddled up to him.

"That was amazing, though," he said.

"I hope I wasn't too rough," Lucas said, carefully looking him over for any signs that he may have hurt him, and found a couple of faint scratches near Elijah's hips. His ears dipped apologetically. "I'm afraid I got a little carried away," he said, lightly rubbing them to try and soothe the redness there.

"I don't even feel them," Elijah told him reassuringly, and then giggled when Lucas touched a ticklish spot near where his leg and groin met.

Lucas smiled at his reaction.

"Like that do you?"

"It tickles but feels so great," Elijah said. His breathing had increased again, and he tried to stay perfectly still despite how much it tickled, even opening his legs slightly to encourage Lucas to touch more of him.

"I was afraid that I might have hurt you when my knot went in," Lucas said quietly.

"Is that what it was?" Elijah asked, cringing slightly at the memory of Lucas's final thrust and feeling something huge enter him all of a sudden.

Lucas nodded, still running his finger over this newly discovered sensitive area on Elijah's body.

"God, I felt so full all of a sudden," Elijah said. "But after the shock of it and the pain went away, it felt so wonderful. I could feel it really pulsing inside me."

"I love you, Elijah. I only ever want you to feel good."

"I love you, too, Lucas, so very much."

Lucas lifted Elijah's chin gently with a clawed finger and slid his tongue softly into Elijah's mouth, giving him a kiss so passionate, Elijah would not soon forget it.

Elijah responded by pulling Lucas closer to him and returning the kiss with just as much passion. He could feel himself responding again to Lucas. But he was too tired and instead let him go and lay his head down on Lucas's chest. He promptly began to fall asleep to the steady, strong sound of

Lucas's beating heart.

The rest of the week was almost a blur to Elijah, except when he was in school. That dragged on as usual Many times he would find himself sitting in front of the maturation chamber with Thomas and Nelle watching Aurora floating inside, fascinated with the whole process of her becoming a Kindred. He could detect no discernable changes in her appearance as of yet, but Per had assured them that they were occurring, even if they could not be seen yet.

When Saturday rolled around, it was Elijah's time to go into the maturation chamber so that the last of his treatment could be completed. Since Per only had one chamber in his home, and that one was occupied, a second unit had to be used. The only available chamber available was one Per kept in his lab at the university. It was strictly off limits to all but a few trusted people. Not even the dean of the university had access to it.

Elijah was nervous about going into the chamber. The last time he was in it he had already been unconscious and unaware of what was happening until he woke up that morning in a strange bed and in a strange house. It was only Lucas's presence—sitting in a chair to watch over him—that had kept him from freaking out.

Again it was Lucas that managed to calm him down. Elijah still had his fears, but just knowing that Lucas would be watching over him made him feel much better.

"I'll see you in two days, Elijah," Lucas said to him.

Elijah gave Lucas one final kiss before he felt the drugs Per had given him begin to take effect. He closed his eyes and let out a deep breath before sleep took him.

Lucas helped Per gently place Elijah into the maturation

chamber. His rebreather was functioning as it should, ensuring Elijah had plenty of oxygen, and the intravenous line was securely inserted into his arm.

He looks so peaceful, Lucas thought.

Just as Aurora had done, Elijah's body naturally curled itself up into a foetal ball.

The way Per had described it to him, entering the maturation chamber was similar to being in the womb. The body remembers this and instinctively causes itself to curl up into the foetal position. It was an entirely subconscious act and not something a person did by choice.

By the second day, Elijah's vitals and the treatment's progress all indicated that everything was proceeding as it should. His heart rate was slightly elevated but otherwise was normal.

Lucas was about to leave the lab to return to the house to check on Aurora's progress, when he suddenly felt a strong feeling of panic come over him. He looked back at the maturation chamber and gasped with alarm. Somehow Elijah had awoken and was in incredible pain. Lucas could see it in his panicking eyes as he started to thrash about in the chamber.

Hitting the alarm, which Per had installed prior to installing the maturation chamber to alert him should anything happen while he was away, Lucas rushed to the chamber to try and get Elijah's attention.

The door to the lab swung open, and Per, slightly out of breath, hurried into the room. He took one look at the tank and saw immediately what was wrong.

"Dammit!" he swore as he moved to the console.

"What's wrong, Dad?" Lucas asked, suddenly very afraid for Elijah, who looked to be in obvious pain.

"His IV has somehow become clogged. It's preventing

the drug that keeps him asleep from entering his system.

"Can he come out of the chamber?"

Per shook his head, studying the readings on the console.

"It's too soon yet. We need to get that line unclogged, now."

Lucas didn't hesitate. He stripped off his clothes and leaped up to the top of the chamber with ease. Opening the lid he dived right in.

Somehow he was able to calm Lucas down enough to allow him access to the intravenous line. Up close, he could see where the problem was. Somehow the line had become wedged between his arm and rib cage, which compressed the tube. Slowly, and as carefully as he could, he extricated the tube and checked it for any breaks. Seeing none, he hurried to the surface, where Per helped him out of the chamber.

With the tube now free of the obstruction, the drug again began to flow into Elijah. Very soon, he was once again asleep.

Lucas was trembling, not because he was cold from being wet, but because of how frightened he had been for Elijah. Nothing like that had ever happened before. Tears filled his eyes as he stared at Elijah, now sleeping comfortably.

"I'm so sorry, Elijah," he whispered, touching the glass with his hand.

"It's not your fault, Lucas. Don't think it was," Per said.

"I made him a promise, Dad, to watch him while he was in there. I should have seen that the line had become tangled."

"But it did, and you caught it," Per said, putting an arm around Lucas. "You were there for him, just as you promised you would be. You didn't fail him."

"Dad, I didn't see the line get tangled. I-I felt Elijah waking up and panicking," Lucas said quietly, almost whispering.

Per looked at Lucas, his head cocked to one side.

"Is this the first time this has happened?" he asked.

Lucas shook his head.

"A few times we were able to hear each other, in our minds. We meant to tell you the other day about it, but with all the excitement over Aurora, we completely forgot."

It would be another seven hours later before it was time for Elijah to come out of the maturation chamber. Per clamped off the intravenous line, stopping the flow of the sedative going into Elijah's system.

Lucas leaped to the top of the chamber to open the lid, just as he had before, and carefully lifted Elijah out of the tank and carried him down. Per was waiting for him with a towel which he wrapped around Elijah. Lucas then lifted him up onto a gurney carefully.

While Lucas waited for the sedative to wear off he used the towel to lightly dry him off, being extra careful not to cause him any discomfort since he knew Elijah would still be a little tender after the procedure.

Elijah soon began to regain consciousness, letting out a soft moan as he shifted slightly on the gurney. Lucas, who had taken a seat next to him, stood up and took a hold of his hand, gently rubbing it as Elijah came round.

"That's it, Elijah, come back to me," Lucas encouraged him quietly.

Slowly Elijah began to open his eyes, but had to blink back against the harsh fluorescent lights above him. As soon as his eyes finally adjusted, though, he looked over to Lucas and smiled up at him.

"Hello, sexy," he said.

Lucas laughed with both relief and happiness, and wrapped his arm around him.

"I'm so sorry, Elijah," Lucas said into Elijah's shoulder.

"Whatever for?" Elijah asked, confused by Lucas's sudden and unexpected apology.

"For not recognizing that you were in trouble."

"I was?"

Lucas stood up straight, and looked at Elijah with surprise.

"You don't remember?" he asked.

"I remember having this really weird dream where I ended up tied up by my arms and legs to some horses who were trying to pull me apart. But that's it until I woke up just now."

"Your IV line had somehow become blocked and you were starting to wake up because the sedative was no longer getting into your system. You were in so much pain you started thrashing about."

Elijah frowned. He could not remember any of that happening at all.

"But you were there to help me, weren't you?" he asked.

Lucas nodded.

"I had to jump in to fix your line."

"Then you have nothing to be sorry about."

"You're amazing, did you know that?" Lucas asked with a wide, toothless grin.

"I know, but it's nice to be reminded, thanks."

Lucas laughed and then leaned down to give him a little kiss. Elijah, however, wanted more. He reached up and wrapped his arms around Lucas's neck to pull him in for a longer, much more passionate kiss. It was only the sound of Per clearing his throat that caused them to separate.

"I guess there's no need to ask how you're feeling, Elijah," Per said with a hint of laughter in his voice.

"Lucas told me what happened," Elijah said.

"You gave us both quite a scare for a bit there."

"Could I get something to drink please?" Elijah asked. "My throat is really starting to bother me all of a sudden."

Lucas hurried to get some water while Per took a seat in the chair beside Elijah.

"Lucas tells me you and him have been hearing each other in your minds," Per said.

Elijah nodded hesitantly, wary about how Per might react.

"One of the traits I wanted to enhance for the Kindred was their sense of perception. Of course I was impressed when we put them through the initial trials, but I am completely at a loss to explain this sudden telepathic ability the two of you seem to have developed."

"It doesn't happen often, but I think I'm actually starting to get used to it when it does."

By now Lucas had returned with a tall glass of water, which he handed to Elijah and was accepted gratefully. Elijah took a very large drink from the glass, almost completely drinking the entire glass.

Thank you, he thought to Lucas.

You're welcome.

"There, it just happened again."

"What just happened exactly?" Per asked, curious.

"I just thanked Lucas for the drink."

"And I told him he was welcome," Lucas finished.

Per looked between Elijah and Lucas. He was very intrigued by this new development.

"Elijah, have you ever in the past thought you heard anyone else's thoughts?" he asked.

"Once, when I was little, I was playing softball when I thought I heard my dad praising me for getting a hit. When I asked him about it after the game, though, he seemed genuinely surprised. We never spoke of it again, though. I think it made him feel uncomfortable."

Per nodded in understanding.

"If the neither of you mind, I'd like to test you both to see how sensitive you are to each other," he said.

Elijah looked at Lucas who nodded his assent.

"Okay," Elijah readily agreed.

He actually wanted to know himself. He thought it would be interesting to see if one day they would be able to carry on a conversation as though they were talking from a distance.

Elijah took another big satisfying gulp of the water, emptying the glass completely. It did soothe his throat a little, but only for a short time. He was also beginning to feel a little groggy as well.

Lucas offered him another glass, which Elijah readily agreed, thanking him again.

"Do you think we can go home now?" Elijah asked. "I'd like to see how Aurora is doing and then I'd like to lie down for a while. I'm feeling a little tired right now."

Per nodded while smiling.

"Of course, that's perfectly understandable. You'll need at least a day to rest anyway so your system can adjust to the changes," he said. "I'm glad to see that you think of the house as your home."

"It feels like it, Doc," Elijah admitted.

"Good, because it is your home now, if you'd like," Per said as Lucas returned with more water for Elijah. "Drink your water so you can get dressed and I'll take you both home."

Elijah smiled when Per said that and quickly did as he was instructed. He was very anxious to get home and very happy now to actually have a place he could finally call home.

I'm going home, he thought excitedly.

Yes, you are.

ELEVEN

E lijah stood in front of the maturation chamber, staring at Aurora floating inside with awe. In the two weeks she had been placed in the tank, she had undergone a remarkable, and dramatic, transformation that fascinated him. Every day seemed to bring something new for him to discover.

Two weeks before, when he had first arrived back home with Lucas and Per after his own brief period in a second chamber, Aurora looked largely like she had the day they met her in the hospital. Several days had passed though, and there were some subtle signs of the Kindred she was soon to become.

A light dusting of fur could be seen beginning to grow in. It lacked any real colour yet but there were some hints of orange and black stripes. From between her legs, sticking out and curling loosely around her was the beginning of a tail growing out from the base of her spine. It had no fur, and looked to Elijah more like a rat's tail. It was long and thin. Her face still looked the same, but he could see that her ears had drawn back slightly and were rounded and erect.

Now, two weeks later, he could see her in her final form. The fur on her body had grown in fully, her mouth and nose had grown outward, forming a short muzzle that revealed two lines of very sharp, imposing-looking teeth. Her arms and legs had grown longer, becoming thin but powerful-looking. Her hands and feet turned into large paws with fingers that ended in sharp, retractable claws.

Nelle was standing with him, watching her daughter intently. She had been equally as fascinated with her daughter's transformation as Elijah was, and rarely moved from her seat as she did not want to miss a single moment of it, only doing so to eat and sleep and take care of her personal needs.

Elijeah, of course, still had school to attend to. By now he had completely caught up with his classwork, and in some ways had even advanced farther than his classmates, taking on extra assignments to try and earn as good a grade as he good. He had been given a new lease on life and he did not want to waste it. Plus he felt by putting every effort into his schoolwork, he was in some small way repaying Lucas and Per for all the help they had given him.

Elijah's love for Lucas grew in this time. There seemed to be no limits for them. They had also learned to communicate quite well telepathically. No longer did their voices in their minds sound muted, but were now as clear as though they were speaking to each other from only a few feet. Distance did not seem to matter, either. Several times when Elijah was in school, working on one of his assignments, when Lucas playfully entered his mind. Each time he had to suppress a moan of pleasure as his body involuntarily, and instantly, reacted to Lucas's touch. He was sure, however, that Kiku had caught him once, as she giggled quietly from her desk.

The maturation chamber itself did not need a lot of attending to by Lucas or Per while Aurora was inside. It was largely self-sustaining, requiring only minute adjustments by Per every now and then. Of course, each time an adjustment was made, Nelle was there asking if anything was wrong, and each time she had to be reassured that Aurora was just fine.

The day finally came when Aurora was ready to come out of the tank. It was a Saturday and both of her parents were present when Lucas, with his incredibly strong legs, leaped up onto the top of the chamber to open the lid. When he gently pulled her out of the tank, still unconscious, he handed her down to her father. Nelle stood by closely with a towel. As soon as Aurora was in her father's arms, Nelle immediately wrapped the towel around her and began drying her fur.

Elijah could now clearly see the colouring of her fur as it no longer was obscured by the greenish fluid in the tank. Lucas had been right. She was a beautiful tiger. He could see it in both her parent's eyes that they thought so, too. Both of them had proud smiles on their faces as Thomas cradled his Kindred daughter in his arms.

Per brought up a gurney whereupon Thomas gently set her down and helped to remove the rebreather that still covered her face. Per then carefully removed her intravenous line.

Before long, after some coaxing by Nelle, Aurora slowly began to come around.

"Hi mom," she said weakly, her voice sounding a little hoarse.

Elijah could sympathize. His own throat had hurt when he emerged from the chamber, but thankfully Per had purchased for him some throat lozenges that really helped, though they tasted a little bitter to him.

"How do you feel, sweetie?" Nelle asked.

Aurora frowned as she stared down at herself. She was still naked, but with all the fur that now covered her she was not self-conscious about it.

"My arms and legs hurt and my throat is sore," she replied.

Elijah knew what she needed and hurried to the nearby sink to get her some water. He offered it to her which she accepted gladly, drinking it almost as quickly as he had filled it.

"It's going to take Aurora a few days to adjust to her new body," Per said, "and she's going to be very tired for the first few days as well."

"What about her leukemia?" Thomas asked.

Per smiled at him reassuringly.

"The readings show it's gone. She's completely cancer free."

"Oh thank you so much, Doctor," Nells said, tears of joy all at once streaming down her face as she embraced him suddenly.

Slightly taken aback by this show of affection, Per simply held her and patted her back lightly until, blushing with embarrassment, she let him go.

"Hey, I look really neat. I'm really a tiger," Aurora said, looking down at herself more closely now that she was more awake.

"Would you like a mirror to see yourself?" Elijah asked.

Aurora nodded enthusiastically.

Elijah hurried to the lab's sink where he carefully lifted the mirror that had been hanging on the wall above it and brought it over to her, pointing the mirror at her so that she could get a good look at herself.

They all watched as Aurora carefully touched her face, feeling her fur, her muzzle and her new, very sharp teeth, and even her ears

"Ouch!" she exclaimed suddenly as she inadvertently nicked the skin on her ear with one of her claws.

Per rushed to get some antiseptic wipes which he then gently applied to her ear. There was no bleeding, but Elijah could definitely see where she had scratched herself just inside the ear where there was no fur to protect her skin.

"You'll have to learn to watch your new claws, Aurora. They can come out when enough pressure is applied to the pads of your fingers," Per told her gently.

"Okay," she nodded in understanding.

Per moved aside to allow Nelle to take over cleaning the wound.

"Both of you will also need to learn your daughter's new needs," Per said to Nelle and Thomas. "It's not just her outward appearance that has changed, but also how she will react to certain stimuli."

"How do you mean?" Nelle asked, looking back at him.

"For one thing your daughter will mature sexually much faster than she would have as a human," Lucas said.

"How much faster exactly?" Thomas asked.

"That depends, really, on whether or not your daughter has begun puberty yet. If she hasn't, she will very soon. By the time she is twelve she will have been in heat at least once," Lucas answered. "The good news for you, though, is that she will only be in heat once every four to six months instead of every month like a human would."

"Wow, I didn't know any of that," Elijah said. Clearly he had a lot to catch up on. But he was sure with Lucas's help he would learn a lot about the Kindred and their peculiarities.

"It's not something normally discussed, except within the family," Lucas said.

"Her libido will also be very strong, and you should prepare yourselves for the fact that she will likely be sexually active much earlier than you expected," Per continued.

Elijah nodded in understanding.

"But because she will only be in heat every few months or so, there won't be a significant chance of her getting pregnant. And, of course, she's immune to any sexually transmitted diseases now, too," he said.

"Exactly," Per nodded, impressed and pleased that Elijah had caught on so quickly.

"This is quite a lot to take in," Thomas admitted.

"Oh there's lots more, but you'll get used to it quickly enough," Lucas laughed. "My dad certainly did."

"I had no choice," Per said.

Aurora chose at that moment to sit up, letting the towel she had been wrapped in to fall off her shoulders. She then swung her legs over the side of the bed, kicking her feet playfully and giggling with amusement as she studied how they looked. Then, before anyone could stop her, she tried to hop off the bed. Unfortunately, in her weakened state, her legs were unable to fully support her wait, and they buckled. She almost fell, but was luckily caught in time, and held steady, by Thomas before she could.

"Easy there, Aurora. You're not yet used to using your new legs," Lucas cautioned her. "Once you've rested up a bit and feel stronger we'll help you learn to use them."

"Okay," she said. Some of her enthusiasm had waned, but she remained smiling nevertheless.

Suddenly she let out a tremendous yawn.

"Looks like you're ready for bed," Nelle said.

Aurora reluctantly nodded. She did not really want to go to bed, but then tried to stifle another yawn, and failing completely.

"Say goodnight to everyone, Aurora, and I'll tuck you into bed," Thomas said, knowing he would likely have to carry her.

Aurora first went to Elijah, walking on unsteady legs, and gave him a hug. She did the same with Lucas and then Per, thanking each of them in turn for helping her become a Kindred and making her well again.

After finally saying goodnight to her mother with a hug and a kiss, Thomas lifted her up into his arms, noticing for the first time that she was much heavier from all the extra muscle she had developed when becoming a Kindred. She wrapped her arms around his neck, her legs around his waist and rested her head on his shoulder as he carried her out of the lab to the bedroom they had been given during their stay at the house. It had, in fact, been Elijah's room until he began sleeping with Lucas.

Back in the lab, Nelle was thanking Per again for everything he and Lucas had done for them.

"It was our pleasure, I assure you," Per said. "We're just glad that she finally gets to have the chance to be a kid again."

"Just keep in mind that as she recovers she'll be one very hungry Kindred, and wanting to eat a lot," Lucas told her before she too left the lab.

"You mean more than she already use to before she got sick?" Nelle laughed.

"Just like a certain teenage boy I know," Per said, pointedly looking at Elijah.

Elijah, though, just snickered lightly in response.

When Elijah woke up the next morning he was greeted with the completely unexpected face of Aurora hovering over him, her wide smile showing her gleaming white teeth. He was momentarily started to find her in bed with him and Lucas, but then smiled back at her.

"Aurora, what are you doing in here?" he asked quietly, not wanting to disturb Lucas.

Too late, I'm awake, he heard Lucas say in his mind.

Elijah looked over to see Lucas staring up at Aurora.

"Couldn't sleep, and I'm hungry," she replied.

Seeing that Lucas was awake also, she lay down between them and snuggled into him. With a chuckle, Lucas pulled the covers over her. He looked at the clock on the bedside table and saw that it was only just past five in the morning.

"It's too early to be awake," he groaned wearily.

But then there was a quiet knock on their door.

"Come in," Lucas called out, opening his eyes again.

The door opened slightly and Elijah could see Nelle in her nightgown poking her head in through the door.

"I just checked on Aurora and she's not in bed," she said with a hint of concern in her voice.

"I'm in here, Mom," Aurora said, sitting up.

Nelle opened the door fully and stepped into the room.

"What are you doing in here, Aurora? You know you shouldn't be bothering Lucas and Elijah like that," she admonished the girl. "I'm really sorry about this, you two," she said to Elijah and Lucas.

"It's okay, Mrs. Avery. We were awake anyway. I just didn't expect to be staring into the face of a tiger when I woke up is all," Elijah said with a giggle.

"I was hungry and you and Dad wouldn't wake up, so I came to see if Lucas and Elijah were awake," Aurora explained innocently.

"Next time knock before going into someone else's room, alright?" Nelle said.

"Okay, Mom," Aurora said, accepting her mother's rebuke.

She then extricated herself from under the covers and carefully climbed over Elijah, trying not to step on him in the process, to sit on the edge of the bed, facing her mother.

"Can I get something to eat now?" she asked.

"Aurora, where is your nightgown?" Nelle asked, aghast that Aurora had come into the room and joined Elijah and Lucas in bed without any clothes on.

"It's too tight, Mom, and I can't put my underwear and pants on because of my tail."

Elijah chuckled at the child's predicament.

"I think you're going to need to do some shopping for Kindred clothes today," he said.

"In the mean time, I think I have an older pair of shorts that don't fit me any more that she can use," Lucas added as he threw off the covers to get out of bed, and started walking to his dresser.

Nelle gasped in shock suddenly behind him.

"Doesn't anyone in this house wear clothing?" she asked with alarm.

Lucas looked back at her as he took his shorts out of the dresser and then gave them to Aurora. She quickly put them on, asking Nelle to help her do up the button at the back above her tail.

"Kindred generally don't like to wear clothing because it can pull at our fur, which is really uncomfortable," Lucas explained to Nelle. "When we do, we prefer to wear something that hugs our bodies tightly. Also for us Kindred with tails, it's important to remember that they remain free of obstructions, since we rely on our tails to help us with our balance."

"I hadn't considered that," Nelle admitted. "Thank you."

"Don't mention it," Lucas said.

"Mom, I'm still hungry," Aurora complained.

"I guess I should start the coffee since I don't think I'm going to be getting any more sleep," Nelle said with a reluctant sigh. "What would you like for breakfast, dear?" she asked Aurora.

"Bacon and eggs!" Aurora answered excitedly, hopping off the bed in anticipation. She was still not used to walking yet, and had to grab for her mother to steady herself when she did.

Elijah had to suppress another chuckle as he swore he could actually hear Aurora's mouth watering in anticipation.

TWELVE

Breakfast that morning with Aurora was certainly different. Although she was in a physically exhausted state, she nevertheless was filled with the seemingly boundless energy typical of a normal nine-year-old child. She could barely sit still in her chair, even when voraciously devouring not just one, but two servings of bacon and eggs. It was all Nelle could do to keep up with her daughter's appetite—despite Per helping her.

Even though Nelle had prepared some toast as well for Aurora, she had only taken a few tiny bites before pushing it aside. This surprised Nelle, as Aurora in the past had been an ardent fan of peanut butter on toast in the mornings. It was not until Lucas explained to her that as a tiger Aurora was primarily carnivorous now, so breads and vegetable matter, and even fruit, would not appeal to her much, if at all, that Nelle understood. It was not something she had considered and had to completely revise her planned shopping list.

As Lucas and Per had expected, shortly after Aurora had finally finished eating, she quickly started to become very tired. She yawned deeply several times, and was having difficulties keeping her eyes open.

Since Elijah had finished eating, he volunteered to help her to bed. Aurora, however, did not want to be left alone. So Per suggested that Elijah take her instead to the living room where he could set her down on the loveseat to sleep.

Even in her tired state she managed to hold on tight to Elijah as he carried her out of the kitchen to the living room, where he gently set her down on the loveseat. She very quickly curled up into a little ball and promptly fell into a deep sleep. He smiled down at her just as Lucas arrived with a blanket which he placed over top of her. Aurora tugged the blanket close to her body to keep herself warm instinctively in her sleep. Giving her an affectionate scratch behind the ear, Elijah then retired to the couch opposite her with Lucas where they sat down and cuddled in each other's arms.

Thomas joined them soon after with his cup of coffee, leaving his wife in the kitchen to help Per with the dishes. He sat down with his coffee in the chair next to the loveseat, placing his coffee on the end table that separated them.

Nelle and Per then came in from the kitchen, having placed all the dishes in the dishwasher and turning it on. While Per took his customary seat in the old chair next to the fireplace, Nelle sat with her daughter on the loveseat, carefully lifting her prone body so that she could sit down, and then rest Aurora's head on her lap. Elijah was impressed that she could do that without waking her up. Aurora simply stirred a little in her sleep, but that is all.

Nelle caught Elijah staring at her and smiled.

"You're really good with children, Elijah," she said. "I

don't think I've seen Aurora be so comfortable with someone that she would allow them to pick her up like you did."

"I've always liked children," Elijah said, blushing slightly from her praise. "Of all the people I've known, it is children that I have found to be the most genuine."

Thomas smiled knowingly.

"It really is a shame all the baggage that we adults burden our children with as they grow older. As children, they know no hatred for anyone and have no prejudices. They learn those from us," he said.

"Have you ever thought to become a father yourself one day, Elijah?" Nelle asked.

Elijah frowned sadly.

"Yeah, once when I was little. I thought about how much love my parents were showing me and I knew that one day I wanted to have a family too and share with my children that same love. But I pretty much was forced to give up that dream when I learned I had AIDS and was dying," he said. "Plus, being gay, it's a given that I won't be able to have children of my own."

I'd give you one if I could, Lucas thought to him.

Elijah heard it and smiled at him.

Although Lucas was trying to cheer Elijah up, he could actually feel the pain that was in Elijah's heart. He really did want to have children of his own some day, but since neither of them were able to conceive it was not really an option for them. Only through adoption or surrogacy could they have a child together, neither of which option Lucas knew Elijah was particularly fond of. He wanted it to be both their children. Lucas made it a point to discuss it with his father sometime in the future.

"Did you need any help shopping for clothes for Aurora,

Mrs. Avery?" Lucas asked, abruptly changing the subject and hoping it would distract Elijah.

"That's very kind of you to offer, Lucas. I don't know the first thing about Kindred clothing, I'm afraid, so I would appreciate any help you can give me."

"I would like to come too, if it's alright," Elijah said.

Lucas thought he still sounded a little down, but there was a hint of excitement in his voice as he thought about doing something for Aurora.

"Of course you can, Elijah," Nelle said.

Elijah excused himself and headed upstairs, knowing he needed to change out of his pajamas if was going to the store with Lucas and Nelle. He was sure Kiku would not mind, though. She would probably think it cute. When he entered the bedroom, though, instead of changing, he found himself standing at the window and staring outside. He did not even hear the door to his room open and Lucas walk in.

"Are you okay, Elijah?" Lucas asked quietly.

Elijah turned to face him. There were tears in his eyes.

"I'm sorry, Lucas. I'd forgotten how much I'd wanted to have children of my own some day," he said. "And then I was holding Aurora in my arms and I really didn't want to let her go. I wanted it to be me on that loveseat caring for her like her mother was."

Lucas stepped up to him as the tears in Elijah's eyes started falling down his cheeks. He really could not stand to see Elijah in pain. He put his arms around him in a tight embrace and rubbed his back comfortingly as Elijah sobbed into his chest.

"I think Mrs. Avery was right. You would make an awesome father some day. And I was serious when I said if I could give you a child, I would."

"I know," Elijah whispered, managing to get his sobbing

under control.

Lucas let him go and held him at arm's length to look deep into his tear stained face. He was relieved to see Elijah give him an almost imperceptible smile of appreciation.

"Come on, let's get changed. We have some shopping to do for a little girl," Lucas said, smiling back at him.

"Now I wish I had some money of my own. I'd like to get her something."

"You pick whatever it is you want to get for her and I will buy it. It can be from the both of us," Lucas said.

Elijah nodded reluctantly.

"What I really need to do is to start looking for a job," he said.

"You could always become one of my dad's lab assistants," Lucas suggested hopefully. Then they'd always be together.

He was not expecting Elijah's reaction, though, which was to laugh.

"Science was always one of my worst subjects in school. I only took it in grade nine because it was a prerequisite course, and I barely passed that with a C- grade."

"Was there something you were interested in doing, then?"

"The only thing I was really any good at, and what I loved before I became sick, was swimming."

"That's perfect, then!" Lucas suddenly beamed. "The university is always on the lookout for strong swimmers to help out around the pool. They're mostly looking for lifeguards for when the elementary school students use the pool. and during the summer when the pool is open to the public." And they'd still get to be together in the same place.

"That does sound cool," Elijah said, finally cracking a

real smile. But then he frowned again. "Oh, but it's been so long since I've been in a pool, and I'm sure I'm really out of shape."

"Well, we do have a pool in the backyard. Dad was going to open it soon and I'm sure you'll be able to use to build up your strength and stamina again."

Elijah smiled enthusiastically as he and Lucas began to get changed. When they left their room together, he was feeling much better than he had when he came in.

By some strange coincidence, when they returned to the living room Aurora was wide awake and clearly excited about something. It did not take them long to discover the reason why, though.

"You guys are so slow!" she exclaimed breathlessly, bouncing off the couch to land in a squat in front of them. "Come on, let's go shopping!"

"Aurora, calm down!" Nelle admonished her daughter, though Elijah caught the brief flicker of a grin tugging at the corner of her lips.

Per was trying hard not to laugh at Aurora's enthusiasm, it reminding him of how Lucas had been when he was growing up, while Thomas was shaking his head, but with a grin on his face. It had been so long since he last saw his daughter this excited and full of energy. He was torn between wanting to scold her for jumping on the furniture and cheering her for how gracefully she had landed.

You could always do both.

Startled, Thomas looked around him to see who had spoken, but saw only Elijah looking at him with a sort of wry smile. Elijah quickly looked away, though, turning his attention to Aurora.

"I know, Mom, but I just feel like I want to run!" Aurora said.

"I know all too well that feeling, Aurora," Lucas laughed.

"Yeah, he loves to run, too," Elijah added.

"See?" Aurora said, looking back at her mother.

Nelle's smile finally cracked, and she even let out a little chuckle.

"You can play all you want outside after we get back," she said.

"Okay," Aurora agreed with a nod.

"Do you mind if I can call Kiku from my class to join us? I'm sure she would know better than any of us what Kindred girls like to wear these days," Elijah asked.

"Is she Kindred too?" Nelle asked.

Elijah nodded and smiled.

"She's a lioness, and we've become pretty good friends recently."

Nelle looked at Elijah with confusion, cocking her head to one side.

"Up until a couple of weeks ago Elijah didn't associate much with any Kindred because his mother forbade him to have anything to do with us," Lucas explained.

Nelle gasped in shock, her eyes opening wide.

"Why in heaven's name not, Elijah?"

"My father left my mom for a male gorilla. Since then she's hated both Kindred and gays," he explained. "It's why she kicked me out of her house."

Nelle shook her head in disbelief.

"I can't understand how some people could have that much hate in their hearts," Nelle said. "Of course she can come if she wants. I think I'm going to need all the help I can get as I get used to Aurora being Kindred now."

Elijah excused himself to place the phone call to Kiku. She had given him her number several days back while they were resting outside during their lunch period. When he finished he found Nelle, Aurora and Lucas already getting ready to leave.

"Kiku suggests we visit Sirens at the Central City Shopping Centre," Elijah said to Nelle, slipping on his shoes that were by the front door. "She'll probably be there by the time we arrive."

Aurora had a problem. Elijah could see that she was trying to put on her shoes, but, of course, they would not fit her feet because she was now Kindred.

"My shoes won't fit me anymore," she said.

"Don't worry, Aurora. Kindred don't need shoes," Lucas assured her. "Besides, I think you'll like going barefoot. It's fun."

Aurora smiled at him, and even giggled a little at the thought of running through a mall without any shoes on. She had always wanted to try that. In fact there were many things she had wanted to try, but never was able to. *Going without clothes was definitely one of them*, she thought as she adjusted the shorts she was wearing to try and lessen her discomfort. She was only partially successful.

Elijah was not at all surprised when Lucas told them he would meet them at the mall. Nelle was confused for a moment, but then smiled as realization dawned on her that Lucas would be run instead. She watched as Elijah gave him a very loving, but still chaste and civilized, kiss before climbing into the car.

Not wanting to wait a moment longer, Lucas sprinted down the driveway to the front gates and rapidly picking up speed.

Aurora complained that she wanted to run with Lucas

too, but Nelle was cognizant of the fact that, despite her eagerness, Aurora was still recovering and there was no way she would be able to run all the way to the mall. She had to remind Aurora of that fact, and although Aurora did not like it, she grudgingly accepted that she would, at least for now, have to travel by car. Her disappointment didn't last, however, because it meant she could ride with Elijah in the back.

They arrived at the mall approximately fifteen minutes later. It took them longer than they expected since the traffic was particularly heavy that morning, even though it was still quite early.

When Elijah got out of the car, he immediately saw Lucas by the mall entrance standing with Kiku and talking to her. He waved to get their attention. They waved back and waited for Elijah to cross the parking lot with Aurora and Nelle.

"Oh you are so beautiful!" Kiku gushed as they approached and she saw Aurora, her ears pricking up immediately, but then frown when she saw that Aurora was walking awkwardly, as though she was just learning to walk.

Had Aurora been human she would be blushing at that moment. As it was though, her ears folded back against her skull slightly from embarrassment.

Kiku took it upon herself to reach out her hand to Aurora so she could help the young Kindred.

Nelle nodded to her appreciatively.

Aurora giggled as she walked hand in hand with the older Kindred into the mall. She looked up at Kiku and studied her face, noticing the resemblance in their faces. They were practically the same except for their colouring.

"You're a lion," Aurora said.

"A lioness, yep," Kiku gently corrected her.

"Cool. I like your tail."

Kiku laughed. Truthfully, she thought her tail was her best feature and was meticulous in keeping it properly groomed.

"Thank you, Aurora. I'll let you brush it one day if you'd like."

"Can I, Mom?" Aurora asked, looking at Nelle.

Nelle smiled and nodded.

"Of course you can, dear. But remember to only brush someone if you know them and they ask you to."

With Elijah holding Lucas's hand, they arrived at the shop Kiku had suggested over the phone that they visit, whereupon they were immediately met by a very friendly male clerk dressed in a semi-formal outfit. He was shaved bald but looked as though he had not shaved his face in a couple of days. It gave him a ruggedly handsome look, Elijah thought. But he was nowhere near as sexy as Lucas. There was something about Lucas's fur that drove him wild.

Maybe I can convince you to brush me later when we get home, he heard Lucas say in his mind.

Elijah smiled and nodded. He loved brushing Lucas's soft fur.

"How are you, Kiku?" the clerk asked, and Elijah was surprised to see them hug. "It's been ages!"

Clearly they were very good friends, which explained to Elijah why Kiku had recommended this particular shop in the first place.

"Oh, busy as ever, Andre. How's the boyfriend?" Kiku asked.

Andre rolled his eyes dramatically.

"That boy is going to drive me to drink, I swear. But he's doing good, thanks."

"Cool, you have a boyfriend too?" Aurora asked. "Lucas and Elijah are boyfriends."

Andre looked down at her and smiled warmly at her.

"Well hello, sweetie, and what's your name?" he asked.

"Aurora."

"Kiku suggested you could help us pick out a new wardrobe for my daughter," Nelle said. "My name is Nelle."

"You have a very beautiful daughter, Nelle," Andre said, shaking her hand.

"Thanks, but I'm still getting used to her being Kindred.

Andre looked at her quizzically.

"She's only recently become Kindred. She was born human. My dad had to make her Kindred to cure her leukemia," Lucas explained.

"You're Lucas, Doctor Wolff's son, aren't you?" Andre asked, his eyes opening wide with recognition.

"And this is my boyfriend, Elijah."

"It's an honour to meet the both of you," Andre practically gushed as he shook both their hands enthusiastically. "My boyfriend is Josef Dahl. I believe you and he trained together, Lucas."

Lucas nodded, recognizing the name.

"Josef was one of the first Kindred, like me," he explained to Elijah. "He's a panther and was in charge of training the Kindred," Lucas explained to Elijah.

"Now he's just a personal trainer, working for Anytime Fitness here in Surrey," Andre said.

"You must love brushing his fur then, like I enjoy brushing Lucas's," Elijah said.

Andre nodded in agreement.

"If I ever need to unwind and relax, all I have to do is offer to brush his fur. And of course he wouldn't say no to a good brushing."

Elijah laughed, remembering well the first time Lucas

had asked him with those pleading eyes to brush his fur.

"So, now let's see about getting this little one some new clothes, shall we?" Andre said, turning his attention back to Aurora.

It took them over an hour to find several sets of clothes that Aurora liked and was moderately comfortable wearing, and that was also acceptable to Nelle. When they finally left the store, saying goodbye to Andre, Aurora was wearing a pair of slim jean shorts cut fairly short, and a tight-fitting, black, sleeveless blouse that crossed over her chest and was tied together at the midriff. It showed a bit of her abdomen, but not obscenely so.

As they exited the mall, Kiku summoned up enough courage to ask Lucas if it would be alright if she came with them to the house for a visit. By her expression, Elijah was sure she was expecting him to say no, and he almost laughed at her expression when Lucas surprised her by saying she could. Elijah was glad for some company. It had been some time since any of his friends had come over to visit. Kenneth had only visited twice more since that first time, and Suzi only once more with Kenneth. He decided he should give them both a call to see if they wanted to get together again some time.

Of course Lucas wanted to run home, but this time he would not be alone, as Kiku chose to run with him.

I'm really going to have to get back into shape so I can run with Lucas also, Elijah thought to himself. He knew if he were to start running with Lucas now, in the shape he was in, without any sort of training or conditioning his body, he would quickly burn himself out.

I will help you if you'd like, Elijah. I would love to go for runs with you, he heard Lucas tell him in his mind.

Elijah smiled and nodded his appreciation, giving Lucas

a kiss before he and Kiku took off sprinting across the parking lot.

Nelle had an easier time driving them back to the house. The traffic was less congested which allowed them to reach the house only a few minutes later. As she turned the car into the driveway and drove it through the front gate, Elijah began to feel uneasy all of a sudden.

They entered the courtyard and Elijah saw another car parked next to Per's. He felt a cold dread in the pit of his stomach when he realized whose car it was.

After Nelle parked behind the new car, Elijah stepped out to see a woman standing by the door engaged in a heated conversation with Per and Thomas.

"Oh no," Elijah said, cringing noticeably.

"What is it, Elijah?" Nelle asked with a look of concern. She held onto Aurora's shoulder protectively, sensing trouble was brewing.

"It's my mother."

THIRTEEN

"What are *you* doing here?" Elijah asked, eyeing his mother suspiciously.

His mother was still a very attractive woman in her early forties. She wore her long, straight, brown hair loose which fell to her shoulders. Elijah knew she had a smile that could melt even the hardest of hearts, which made it all the more creepy that she was smiling at him now.

"That's no way to say hello to your mother," she said.

"It is when the last time we spoke, you threw me out of the house and told me you never wanted to see or hear from me again, Meredith," Elijah said, refusing to even acknowledge her as his mother by calling her by her name.

Meredith's smile faltered a little as she stepped toward him. Elijah held his ground, crossing his arms over his chest.

"I was angry, baby. I didn't mean the awful things I said. It's time for you come home where you belong," Meredith said in a conciliatory voice.

The part of him that still loved his mother wanted to believe her. He wanted to throw himself into her arms and feel once again her warm embrace as she used to when he was little. But his rational mind knew it could not happen.

"No, what you want is to try and make me change who I am for you. Well, I can't do that, Meredith. I won't do that. Not for you, and not for anyone. You forfeited your claim to be my mother when you threw me out of the house. Just go back home."

It was right around then that Lucas and Kiku arrived, running into the courtyard and the both of them panting. Lucas took one look at the situation unfolding before him and right away could feel the growing tension between Elijah and this strange woman who bore a remarkable resemblance to him. He knew that this must be Elijah's mother.

Nelle also could feel the tension building and she hurried a confused-looking Aurora into the house, as it appeared things were going to get a lot more heated really quickly.

"Don't talk to me like that, Elijah," Meredith spat, frowning. It was almost a scowl. "I am legally still your mother and you will leave here at once."

Elijah looked at her incredulously.

"If you think I am going anywhere with you, you're nuts," he said.

"You will do as you are told," she replied, her voice rising in anger.

Lucas quickly moved to stand between Elijah and Meredith, as she suddenly appeared poised to strike him. There was no way that Lucas was going to allow that to happen.

"I suggest you do as Elijah said and leave now," he said, his ears folding back against his skull in anger and his lips curling back in a growl, showing his sharp canine teeth.

Elijah could see Meredith flinch under Lucas's intimidating gaze, but she did not budge an inch from her spot.

"Don't you dare interfere, you damn dirty beast!" she spat with such vehemence that Lucas was momentarily stunned. "You'll regret it if you do."

Lucas's eyes narrowed, menacingly.

"Is that a threat?"

"No, it's a promise," Meredith shot back.

Per, incensed that this woman would openly threaten her son and his, exploded with rage.

"Get your damn, racist carcass off my property, now, or I'll have you physically removed."

Meredith staggered back slightly under the force of his anger, but then she sneered at him before finally storming haughtily away and climbing into her car. She drove off in a cloud of dust, kicked up by her spinning back tires, and was gone.

Elijah stared after her with tears in his eyes.

"I'll go get my things," he said, hanging his head as he started inside.

Lucas quickly stopped him as he reached the door, suddenly concerned.

"Whatever for, Elijah?" he asked, shocked that Elijah was thinking of leaving.

Tears started down Elijah's cheeks as he turned to look into Lucas's face.

"I can't let my mother cause trouble for you and Doc. I love you far too much to allow that to happen. It's best if I just go. Then maybe she'll leave you alone."

"Is that what you really want?"

Elijah shook his head.

"What I want is to stay here with you forever."

"Then stay."

"But my mother—"

"Will regret ever trying to cause problems for us," Lucas told him gently.

"Lucas is right, Elijah. We're a family, now, and families stick together no matter what," Per said.

"Please stay, Elijah," Lucas pleaded with him. "Forever and for always."

"If you're foolish enough to leave, Elijah, I'm never talking to you again," Kiku promised as she stared at him with her arms folded across her chest, speaking for the first time since she and Lucas arrived.

Elijah finally smiled and nodded, prompting Kiku to pump her fist back.

"Yes!" she exclaimed triumphantly.

Elijah and Lucas both laughed. How could they not?

Lucas then drew Elijah into a tight embrace as Elijah suddenly broke down in tears.

"Why does she hate me so much?" Elijah asked between deep, heaving sobs.

Neither Per or Lucas could answer him, though. But it became clear to them both now that Elijah was definitely suffering from acute depression. There was no amount of medication, no easy treatment, to cure him of this ailment like his AIDS had been; only time and lots of patience. And if there was one thing the Kindred were best known for, it was their patience.

Elijah's sobs eventually subsided and he looked at Lucas with embarrassment, blushing noticeably.

"Sorry, I don't know why I'm such a mess all of a sudden," he said, wiping the tears from his face.

Lucas smiled at him reassuringly, taking a hold of his

hand.

"It's perfectly understandable. You've had to go through a lot with your family," he said.

He then opened the door and led Elijah into the house, Per, Thomas and Kiku following close behind them. Once inside Lucas suggested to Elijah that he should try to lie down upstairs to get some rest. But Elijah declined, pointing out that they had guests and he would rather stay with them.

Lucas nodded happily, encouraged by the fact that Elijah appeared to be fighting back against his depression.

He's a fighter for sure, he thought privately.

They stepped into the living room where Nelle and Aurora had been sitting on the couch with a book. Seeing them come in, Nelle looked up at them and saw Elijah's sullen mood. His eyes were red and puffy from crying.

"Why is Elijah so sad?" Aurora asked, looking concerned.

"His mother doesn't like him much because he's in love with Lucas. She said some really mean things to him," Nelle explained.

Aurora frowned, ears flicking briefly.

"Well, that's stupid. I like Elijah. He's fun to be with, and I'm glad he loves Lucas. They look cute together."

Despite his earlier sadness, Aurora's comment made it impossible for him to stop from cracking a huge grin.

"Thank you, Aurora. That really means a lot to me. I like you, too, cub," he said.

Aurora cocked her head to one side as she tried to figure out why Elijah had called her that.

"Oh, God, I've not heard a Kindred child called that in ages," Kiku laughed.

Even Lucas had to laugh at Elijah's little joke. He had

the most refreshing sense of humour.

"Why'd you call me a cub?" Aurora asked, still confused.

Elijah knelt down before her and put his hands on hers.

"Because that's what little tigers are called," he explained with a loving smile.

Aurora finally smiled as she understood.

"That makes you my little cub," Nelle said, holding Aurora close in a tight embrace, causing Aurora to giggle happily.

Did I mention how much I love you?

Yes, but tell me again anyway, Elijah thought back to Lucas, looking up at him.

I love you.

Elijah was quickly beginning to see how much easier it was for them to communicate in each other's minds. He liked that it was something that only he and Lucas shared. Something that they could call their own.

The unexpected and disturbing confrontation with his mother left Elijah a little shaken up. He needed to unwind, or as Lucas suggested, to relax. There was only one thing that he found truly relaxing, and that was to go for a long leisurely swim.

"Doc, do you think there is a chance that I could go for a swim?" he asked, looking at Per hopefully.

Aurora's eyes opened wide with excitement at this. She had no idea that the house even had a pool.

"Say, why don't we all go out back," Thomas suggested. "It's a nice day and it would be a shame to spend it all inside."

There were many nods of agreement all around as everyone thought the idea was a good one.

"I only turned on the pool heater yesterday, Elijah. So

don't expect the water to be too warm yet," Per cautioned him.

Elijah smiled.

"That's okay. I prefer it cool anyway," he assured him.

"Well, you're not getting me into a pool, warm water or not!" Kiku said adamantly.

Lucas laughed knowingly.

"Cats never were all that fond of water. The same has always been true with the feline Kindred as well."

"Mom, can I go swimming too?" Aurora asked, surprising Kiku, Lucas and Per, who all looked at her in shocked amazement.

"You don't have a suit though, sweetie," Nelle reminded her.

Aurora giggled conspiratorially.

"I don't need a suit, I have fur!" she said.

Before anyone could stop her, Aurora began removing her clothing right there in the living room in front of everyone. Elijah could plainly see the relief on her face as each article of clothing was quickly removed. He guessed she had just been waiting for an excuse—any excuse at all—to shed her clothes.

"Aurora, what are you doing? Put your clothes back on this instant!" Nelle exclaimed with alarm, aghast that her daughter was so freely removing her clothing in front of people.

"See, Mom, no one can see anything. It's like I'm wearing a warm fur coat, only it covers everything.

"You'd better get used to it, Mrs. Avery," Kiku said, unable to resist an amused snicker. "Most Kindred will find any excuse to go without clothing if they can."

Nelle shook her head in bewilderment. What she found particularly odd, though, was that her husband had not tried to stop their daughter at all, as though he not only did not see a problem with it but also expected it as well.

"Well, if you're going swimming, I'd better get the pool ready," Per said with a bemused grin, standing up. "But I want to strongly emphasize how important it is that nobody enters the pool unless there is another adult present."

Elijah nodded in agreement. He expected this to be a condition to using the pool. Even the most experienced swimmers can get into trouble in the water unexpectedly. It was a very sensible rule.

Before he could head out to the pool with the others, though, Elijah first had to get changed into his swimming trunks. Unlike the Kindred, he had no fur to protect his modesty. Despite having lost quite a bit of weight, Elijah was pleasantly surprised to discover that his swimsuit actually still fit him, although not as snugly as it did before. His swimsuit was not one of those long shorts popular with teens these days, but rather it was a tight pair of briefs-style Speedos. He preferred them over other swimsuits because they offered him the least amount of resistance in the water. Those baggy shorts can make it more difficult to swim.

When he came back down the stairs, where Lucas had been waiting for him with a couple of large towels, Elijah had to suppress a laugh as Lucas gawked up at him, or more specifically at what he was wearing. A giant smile stretched across the Kindred's face.

I like the suit, Elijah heard in his mind. *You should wear it more often.*

I'm sure you'd be just as thrilled if I was naked.

I wouldn't complain, Lucas admitted with a laugh as he led Elijah out back with an arm around his shoulders.

Just you wait until I get you alone tonight.

Now that's something to look forward to, Lucas thought, playfully licking behind Elijah's ear and making him giggle with delight.

Per was just finishing rolling up the pool cover when they stepped out on the back deck. Thomas and Nelle were drinking some coffee while they sat at the patio table with the wide umbrella above them fully extended to shelter them from the heat from the morning sun. Kiku sat on one of the lounge chairs near the pool. She had put on a pair of sunglasses, while Aurora was staring at the pool, but this time looking less enthusiastic about jumping in.

"Hey, Doctor Wolff, would it be alright if I got more comfortable?" Kiku asked.

Per looked at her, knowing exactly what she was asking to do, and then looked over at Nelle, who also seemed to realize what Kiku wanted.

Nelle shrugged her shoulders indifferently, deciding that Lucas and Kiku were both right. Now that she had a Kindred daughter she was going to have to get used to the Kindred disdain for clothing. She knew how difficult, and ultimately how futile, it was to fight against one's own nature.

"It's fine, Kiku. Go ahead," Per nodded.

Kiku needed no further prompting as she quickly began removing her blouse and then shorts until she stood naked like Aurora.

Elijah watched with fascination at Kiku, who, after getting undressed, casually lay down on the lounge chair with the obvious intent of soaking in the warmth of the sun. He could not help but be intrigued by her as well. Her fur, was absolutely stunningly beautiful, almost glowing in the light of the sun.

"Cat caught your tongue?" Lucas asked, quietly appearing beside Elijah and no longer wearing his clothes either.

Elijah's eyes automatically fell to Lucas's crotch where they lingered hungrily for a moment before he finally looked up into the Kindred's face, and smiled.

She's beautiful, Lucas, he thought to him. *I don't understand why she doesn't have anyone.*

Yes she is. But perhaps she already has what she wants, Lucas suggested.

What do you mean?

Haven't you noticed the way she looks at you sometimes?

Elijah looked at him incredulously.

But I'm gay, she knows that. There's no way I could love her like that. We could only ever be really good friends.

Perhaps it's enough for her to be your friend. But it wouldn't stop her from wishing for something more.

"No, I suppose not," Elijah said aloud, seeing Lucas's point.

He turned from Kiku reluctantly to glance down into the pool. The truth was he had grown very fond of Kiku in the short time they had known each other and thought of her as more than just a friend. She was like a sister to him. Being an only child, Elijah had often wondered what it would have been like to have grown up with a brother or sister ... or both Perhaps if he had, things would have turned out differently between him and his mother.

The water in the pool was so clear that Elijah could easily see the bottom at both ends. At its shallowest, he figured the pool was about three feet deep and at its deepest was about ten feet deep. He knew from experience that the easiest way to acclimate to the temperature of the water was to just jump in. The worst a person could do was to enter the water gradually. It took forever to get used to the water temperature that way. So without any delay, Elijah jumped in feet first, allowing himself to be submerged completely before kicking off from the bottom with his feet to resurface.

The pool was refreshingly cool, just the way he preferred. It was perfect for a morning swim. Then, without warning, he heard a little splash behind him, and he turned in time to catch a brief glimpse of Aurora's head disappearing under the water as she jumped into the pool like he did. No sooner had she resurfaced, though, than she let out a high-pitched yowl before desperately reaching for the side of the pool where she pulled herself clear out of the water as though she was trying to escape a burning fire.

Aurora's mother was right there with a towel for her, wrapping it around the shivering Kindred child, who stared at the water in the pool.

"I'm not doing that again!" Aurora declared as she shook her head to rid herself of the some of the water dripping from her fur.

"Too cold, honey?" Nelle asked.

"Too right!" she exclaimed, looking back at the pool and giving an involutary shudder.

Lucas chuckled with amusement as he then dove cleanly into the pool to join Elijah in the water.

FOURTEEN

Elijah was thoroughly enjoying his swim in the pool. Although it was nowhere near the size of an Olympic-sized swimming pool he was used to, he still managed to get quite a good workout from swimming its length several times before beginning to tire. He frowned slightly as he hung onto the edge of the pool at the deep end.

Lucas saw his frown and swam up beside him, putting his hand on the edge to stay afloat.

"What's the matter, Elijah?" he asked.

"I was only able to swim ten lengths before I got too tired. Before I got sick, I used to be able to swim twice that in a pool of this size."

"Don't be so hard on yourself. It'll take some time before you will get back in shape and be able to swim like you used to," Lucas said.

"What I really need is a trainer, someone who can help me to regain my stamina and build up my muscles."

Lucas smiled.

"I think we both know of the perfect person to ask."

"Who?" Elijah asked, looking at Lucas with renewed excitement in his eyes.

"You remember Andre from the store right?"

"Who could forget him?" Elijah said, remembering the flamboyant clerk.

"Well, he did mention that his boyfriend is a personal trainer now, so maybe you could ask him," Lucas suggested.

"That would be perfect!" Elijah said happily, throwing his arms around Lucas and giving him a kiss on his lips.

Just then Elijah cringed deeply as he felt a sudden sharp and intense pain in his leg as his muscles cramped up. He only just barely managed to cry out. As it was, though, he had to hold on to Lucas to keep afloat.

Lucas reacted immediately, both seeing and feeling that Elijah was in excruciating pain. Holding onto him tightly, he kicked off from the wall and swam as quickly as he could with Elijah to the shallow end where he helped him out of the pool. Once he got out himself, he walked Elijah to one of the lounge chairs and set him down.

From where he sat at the patio table, Thomas also saw that Elijah was in trouble and rushed to his side to see if he could help.

"What's hurting?" he asked Elijah.

"My leg," Elijah gasped through clenched teeth as his leg tightened up even further. "It's a really huge cramp in my right leg."

"Here, let me help you with that," Kiku said getting up from her lounge chair. "My older sister is a marathon runner and I used to massage her muscles for her after a race."

Elijah nodded desperately, willing to try anything to stop

the pain. With Lucas's help he rolled over onto his stomach to give her better access.

Kiku knelt down by his legs. She could easily tell which leg had cramped up by the way his muscles had tightened into a really painful contracted state. She began by applying a gentle massage to the cramped muscle, increasing the circulation of blood to the tissue. Very slowly, the muscle began to respond, and loosened, which in turn began easing Elijah's pain.

"Do you still help your sister out with this?" Thomas asked.

"Nah, she married a massage therapist so he does it for her now," Kiku laughed as she continued relaxing the muscles until they had fully loosened up.

A long sigh of relief escaped from Elijah's lips when the pain had disappeared completely and he was able to move the leg again.

"That sounds like the perfect match!" Thomas said.

"My parents certainly thought so. Plus it doesn't hurt that they're madly in love with each other."

"I'll bet," Elijah snickered.

Kiku's expert ministrations, unexpectedly, had an additional effect on him. She was so good, and he was so relaxed, in fact, that he was beginning to doze off. That is, until Lucas swatted him playfully on his Speedo-clad behind, startling him awake. Behind him he could hear Kiku giggling as she moved down his leg to his calf.

No sleeping, he heard Lucas say in his mind.

Kiku finally finished, allowing Elijah to roll back over and sit up. He tested the leg and smiled at her in gratitude.

"Thank you, Kiku, that was amazing," he said.

That's not the only thing that enjoyed your massage, it seems, Lucas laughed in his mind.

Elijah looked down and immediately his face flushed a deep red with embarrassment when he saw that he was, in fact, tenting in his bathing suit, the Speedo's material accentuating every detail clearly as though he were not wearing anything at all. He quickly folded his arms across his lap, praying that Kiku had not noticed. But she did, and he groaned inwardly when she smiled and winked at him before returning to her chair. To her credit, though, she did not say anything about it.

The rest of that morning, and part of the afternoon, was spent lounging out in the back yard. While Elijah rested, lying on a lounge chair, Lucas rubbed some suntan lotion on his exposed skin to prevent him from getting a sunburn. A couple of times Lucas caused him to squirm when his hand slipped beneath Elijah's Speedos slightly, wickedly teasing him.

Beside him, in the other lounge chair, Kiku lay on her front as Aurora deliriously brushed Kiku's fur. Elijah smiled as he watched when he could clearly hear a loud purring from Kiku who was obviously enjoying the brushing.

It was then, while Aurora continued to brush Kiku's fur, and the adults sat watching them with amusement under the shade of the umbrella at the patio table, that they all heard the unmistakable distinctive sound of the doorbell being rung. It rang once, and then rang a second time.

Per got up from his seat, slightly irritated.

"Now who on Earth could that be?" he wondered out loud before opening the back sliding door and entering the house.

Moments later he returned accompanied by two Kindred. Both were panthers, Elijah saw, an adult male and a small female cub a little younger than Aurora, their short, black fur gleaming in the sun as they stepped out onto the deck. The cub appeared to be quite shy as she mostly hid behind the adult's legs.

"Lucas, someone's here to see you," Per said.

Lucas looked up from Elijah and a wide grin stretched across his face when he instantly recognized the male. He quickly scrambled to his feet to meet them.

"Josef!" Lucas said, welcoming his good friend with a warm embrace.

"It's good to see you again, Lucas," Josef said with a smile. "Andre told me you'd visited the store this morning with your new boyfriend."

"Elijah, this is Josef, Andre's boyfriend," Lucas said as Elijah stood up to join them.

"Very nice to meet you, Elijah. You're a very lucky guy to have captured Lucas's heart."

"Thanks, I certainly think so, too," Elijah said, shaking the Kindred's hand and noting the strength in his grip and his size, which eclipsed Lucas by at least a foot.

Wow, Elijah thought.

I know, huge and strong. But he has a really gentle heart, Lucas said in his mind.

"And who is this with you, Josef?" Lucas asked, looking down at the cub who shied away from him and looked at him with uncertain eyes.

"Her name is Tyra. She's an orphan that Andre and I have begun fostering."

"Well, that certainly explains the comment Andre made about you driving him to drink," Elijah snickered.

"Yeah, I'm afraid I did spring this on him quite suddenly when I called Andre to let him know I was coming home with a Kindred cub," Josef said sheepishly, his ears dipping slightly.

"By the sounds of it, he wasn't too prepared for the news."

"That would be an understatement. I'd only gone to the Children's Aid Society office to hand in our completed applications to become foster parents, when I saw this really sad cub sitting alone by a chair, and an older couple talking to a social worker about her. I didn't like the way the two of them felt, or how they were looking at Tyra, so I asked to foster her on the spot. I think our social worker was glad we did. Apparently she wasn't too pleased with the couple either. But there are so few people wanting to take in Kindred youth. Andre settled down once I explained it to him, and he agreed that it was the right thing to do."

"I would have," Elijah said quietly.

Lucas knew very well Elijah's desire for a child of his own, so he understood how Elijah felt. He had no doubt Elijah would have done the same for Tyra as Josef and Andre, given the chance. The very first opportunity he got, he knew he had to talk to his dad in private about their options in the future. It didn't come as much of a surprise to him then, when Elijah stepped forward and knelt down to the cub's level. He did not approach too closely, though, not wanting to scare her.

"Hello, Tyra, I'm Elijah," he said, giving her a friendly smile.

"Hi," she squeaked hesitantly, peeking out from behind Josef.

Just then, Tyra stiffened up as Aurora cautiously approached, brush in hand. Elijah looked behind him to see that Kiku, somehow, had fallen fast asleep and was completely oblivious to the presence of the two Kindred that had joined them in the back yard.

That had to have been some brushing Aurora gave her, Elijah thought.

Incredible, Lucas replied, following his gaze and seeing

Kiku lying on the lounge chair, snoring softly away.

The way Aurora was walking seemed to concern Tyra, who looked worriedly at her.

"Daddy, I think she's hurt," she whispered up at Josef.

It was loud enough, though, that Elijah could hear her.

"No, it's okay, Tyra. Aurora's not hurt," he assured her. "This is just her first day as a Kindred and she's not used to walking with her new legs, yet."

"Is this true?" Josef asked, looking wide-eyed at Lucas.

Lucas nodded.

"She had the same cancer I did, and dad offered to help her."

"She looks so beautiful. I don't think I've seen a more beautiful tiger," Josef said.

"Thank you," Nelle said who joined them with Thomas.

They shook hands and introduced themselves.

"The two of you must be very proud," Josef said.

"We are, thank you," Thomas nodded. "We're especially grateful to Doctor Wolff for everything he's done for her. While we're still getting used to her as a Kindred, it's just been so great to see her playing and enjoying herself again. The last two years have been really hard on all of us."

"You have my sympathies, both of you. But I'm glad things turned out well for your daughter in the end."

As though oblivious to the conversation going on around her, Aurora held up the brush to Tyra.

"Would you like me to brush your fur for you?" she asked.

Tyra first looked at the brush in Aurora's hand, and then looked up at Josef hopefully.

"Can I, Daddy?" she asked.

Josef nodded while smiling appreciatively at Aurora.

Aurora took hold of Tyra's hand and led her to the lounge chairs. Tyra lay down at Aurora's urging and almost immediately began to purr with pleasure as Aurora began gently brushing her fur.

Tearing his attention away from the two cubs, Josef looked at Elijah, a wry grin forming on his face.

"So, Elijah, how did you do it?" he asked. "How did you manage to get this big lug to fall in love with you?"

"Quite literally, by threatening to throw myself off the New Westminster bridge," Elijah replied.

Josef's eyes widened dramatically, ears pricking with alarm. He looked to Lucas for confirmation who gave it by nodding ever so slightly.

"I was dying with AIDS and since there was nothing the doctors could do for me, I decided to end my life on my own terms and not because of some stupid disease," Elijah explained.

Josef noded in sympathetic understanding.

"I found him during one of my evening walks and convinced him to instead come here where my dad was able to cure him."

"You're a very lucky and brave young man. I don't know many who would have had the courage to deal with what you had to go through the way you did," Per said.

This time Elijah's blush was very noticeable. He could definitely feel it in his face.

And very cute, too, Lucas said in his mind.

"Oh, God," Elijah said quietly, trying to hide his face in his hands which caused Lucas to laugh almost hysterically.

"Did I miss something?" Josef asked, looking from one to the other in confusion.

"For reasons I haven't been able to determine, Lucas and Elijah have developed some kind of telepathic link. We probably just saw the result of one of their private conversations," Per explained.

"Earlier, when we were inside discussing Aurora's sudden aversion to wearing clothing, I thought I heard Elijah talking to me. But it sounded like he was speaking to me from a different room when he was in fact sitting only a few feet from me," Thomas slowly said, uncertain if he should be mentioning it.

Elijah nodded to confirm that he remembered it happening.

"It's strange, because it almost felt as though I was actually experiencing the couple's thoughts at the Children's Aid Society."

"Dad, could this mean the Kindred are beginning to develop a telepathic talent?" Lucas asked, surprised to hear this revelation from Josef.

"It could be, but that wouldn't explain how Elijah seems to be more easily able to communicate with people other than yourself, Lucas."

"Good genes, I guess," Elijah said with a shrug of his shoulders. But then he frowned when it reminded him of his mother. "Probably another thing she'd hate me for."

"The reason Elijah ended up with us, was because his mother kicked him out of the house for being gay and having AIDS," Lucas quickly explained when he saw Josef's shocked expression. "Actually, I should probably thank her, because if it weren't for her, Elijah and I may never have met."

Elijah smiled at that and hugged Lucas.

"Damn, you two have it bad," Josef laughed.

Lucas and Elijah both nodded in agreement as they then shared a brief kiss together.

FIFTEEN

It was not long before Tyra had grown comfortable enough that she soon began frolicking about with Aurora as though they had been playing together all their lives. Being cats, neither of them showed any interest in going into the pool, but Nelle did caution them both not to run on the pool deck as it was slippery and they could get hurt.

Tyra had, in fact, become so comfortable that within a few minutes of playing with Aurora she had already shed her clothing until she was as naked as Aurora was, much to the amusement of the adults. This included Nelle, who by now was growing quite accustomed to the Kindred's aversion toward clothing.

Elijah, deciding he'd had enough sun for a while, convinced Lucas to join him for another, more leisurely swim in the pool. Lucas enthusiastically agreed, although he cautioned Elijah not to push himself so hard that he risked getting another cramp.

They largely stayed in the the shallow end of the pool, soaking in the cool water and occasionally splashing each other playfully with water.

Kiku even decided to join them, though she just sat on the edge of the pool, letting only her legs and feet soak in the water. Elijah and Lucas were both very careful to avoid splashing her due to her dislike of the water.

What completely surprised Elijah and Kiku both, though, was when Josef unexpectedly joined them, stripping off his shorts and shirt, and diving into the pool. Elijah looked at Lucas with bewilderment. Lucas, though, just laughed as Josef resurfaced and swam up next to them at the side of the pool.

"Josef is the only cat I know of who actually loves to swim," Lucas said.

"Can't very well have a soldier commanding troops who is afraid of a silly thing like water, now can they?" Josef said, referring to the time, many years ago, he was responsible for training the Kindred to fight against the terrorists.

"He hated it at first, just like the other cats, but he trained himself daily to first tolerate the water, and then later to enjoy it."

"There's no better exercise for the body than a good swim," Josef said.

"Thanks, but I think I'll pass," Kiku said, to which Josef just laughed.

"Andre said you're a personal trainer now," Elijah said.

"That's right."

"I've just become recently aware of just how out of shape I am because of my AIDS," Elijah said. "Do you think you could help me sometime get back into shape?" he asked.

"Just before you arrived, Elijah was swimming lengths in the pool when he suffered a very painful cramp in his leg,"

Lucas explained.

"I hope to one day soon become a lifeguard for the university, but I know I'd have to pass their fitness tests before I would even be considered for the job," Elijah added.

"You really enjoy the pool, don't you?" Josef asked.

Elijah nodded enthusiastically.

"When I was just a kid, my dad used to call me his little tadpole boy."

Josef laughed, as did Lucas and Kiku, who both thought it was the cutest thing they had ever heard.

"Where is your dad now, if you don't mind me asking?" Josef asked.

"Living in Ottawa with his gorilla boyfriend."

Josef nodded in understanding. Elijah's was not the first family he had seen broken up when on parent fell in love with a Kindred.

"Well, Elijah, I would be happy to help you get back into shape. It's the least I could do for the boyfriend of my best friend. But it'll have to be private session here at the house instead of going to the gym. There you would have to pay to join and receive one on one training with me."

Just then they suddenly heard a frightened yell followed by a splash in the deep end of the pool. Elijah just managed to catch a flash of black before it disappeared under the water.

Before anyone else could react, Elijah kicked off hard from the edge of the pool. Diving under the water, he found Tyra struggling to get back to the surface. He sped toward her, grabbed her by the waist, and then swam back up to the surface with her securely in his arm.

No sooner had they breached the surface, than Tyra began sputtering and coughing up water from her lungs. By then Josef and Lucas had reached them and helped Elijah bring the terrified cub to the side of the pool. Josef then leaped out of the water and pulled Tyra out onto the deck as she began to cry.

Nelle was there with a dry towel which she gave to a grateful Josef. He wrapped Tyra in it and began soothing her while drying her down.

"What happened, Sweetie?" Josef asked.

"I tried to catch the ball, but I slipped," Tyra said between tiny sobs. "Are you mad at me? Do I have to go back to the home now?"

Elijah could see on her face, and the way her ears had dropped, that she was more afraid of what Josef might do than she was falling into the pool. His heart immediately went out to her. Already she had lost her parents and now was afraid that she would lose the only other person who had loved her unconditionally.

"No, Sweetie, I'm not mad at you. It was an accident. I'm just glad that you're safe," Josef assured her softly, pulling her into a comfortable embrace.

He carefully lifted her up, Tyra instinctively wrapping her long legs around his waist, and carried her over to the table where he sat her down on his lap.

As Elijah, Lucas and Kiku followed, Kiku leaned close to Elijah.

"You're really a special guy, Elijah, for saving Tyra like that," she whispered in his ear, and gave him a kiss on his cheek.

Elijah blushed. He certainly did not think he did anything extraordinary, and thought it was just lucky of him to have gotten to her first.

She's right, you know, you are real special, Lucas said in his mind.

Lucas leaned over and planted a kiss on his other cheek.

Still blushing from both of their affectionate praises,

Elijah squatted down a little so he could look Tyra in the eye.

"Are you okay?" he asked her.

Tyra looked at him through tear stained eyes, nodding as a barely perceptible smile tugged at the corners of her mouth.

"But you're afraid your new daddy doesn't love you any more, right?"

Again Tyra nodded, this time with a frown.

"You don't have to be afraid of that," Elijah assured her. "I know for a fact that he loves you very, very much."

Tyra looked at him with uncertain eyes.

"How do you know?"

"Because I can feel how much he loves you," Elijah said. "And so can you."

"How?" she asked, not believing him.

"Go ahead and put your hand on his chest."

At first Tyra hesitated, thinking it odd thing for Elijah to tell her to do, but then pushed back a little and put her hand on Josef's chest.

"Can you feel how strong his heart is beating?" Elijah asked.

Tyra nodded, and smiled.

"That's how strong his love is for you. He will always love you. That will never change, even when you make a mistake."

"I love you too, daddy!" she cried with renewed tears, but happy ones this time, as she pushed herself back into Josef's chest and gripped him in a tight hug.

Josef looked up at Elijah, tears in his own eyes, and smiling widely.

"Thank you," he mouthed to Elijah with great appreciation for what he had done for the both of them.

Out of the corner of his eye, Josef noticed Aurora

standing nearby, the ball she and Tyra had been playing with in her hands, and looking as though she was wracked with guilt. Her ears were flattened in distress, and her tail flicked nervously. He beckoned her to step closer.

She did, hesitantly, refusing to look up at him.

"I'm sorry," she said in a meek voice. "I didn't mean to throw the ball so hard—"

"It's alright, Aurora," Josef said gently, stopping her in mid-sentence to try and convince the frightened Kindred cub that he was not mad at her. "No one is blaming you for what happened, honey."

Thomas then stood up and walked around the table to scoop up Aurora in his arms. Her eyes were moist as she looked at her father with uncertainty, afraid that he might be angry with her. She was surprised then when he smiled at her instead.

"Did you have fun playing with Tyra, Sweetie?" he asked her.

She finally smiled and nodded.

"I like her."

"We can see that," Thomas said. "You just have to be a little more careful next time. You're much stronger than you used to be, okay?"

"Okay," she said, her whole body relaxing as she finally realized she was not in trouble. But then she jerked with a start and looked at him with wide, excited eyes as she suddenly caught on to what he had just said. "You mean I will be able to play with Tyra again some time?" she asked hopefully.

Thomas laughed.

"Of course, if her daddy says it is okay," he said.

Aurora looked back at Josef who nodded his approval. Tyra also appeared to like the idea as she smiled at Aurora.

Seeing as how play time was definitely over, Per cleared

his throat to grab their attention.

"What do you all say to a bit of ice cream?" he suggested.

The two cubs' eyes lit up immediately at the mention of ice cream, both girls wriggling out of their respective fathers' grasps and looking up at Per with mouths hanging open and tongues licking their lips in anticipation as both their tears gave way to drooling mouths.

"Somehow I don't think they need any convincing, Doctor," Nelle said with a mirthful grin.

As the day wore on, the sun beginning its inevitable, slow descent, and evening was soon upon them. They had all enjoyed their bowls of ice cream, the two young cubs even enjoying seconds, and were just relaxing out on the patio while enjoying the cool evening breeze.

Per invited Josef and Tyra to stay over for dinner, but Josef reluctantly declined, claiming the need to get back to their home and to Andre, who would have already returned home from work by now.

Aurora was sad to see Tyra leave, but smiled when she was told she could visit them some time, and, of course, Tyra would no doubt like to visit her as well.

After saying their goodbyes, which included Tyra giving an especially long hug to Elijah as a way of thanking him for saving her, they left. Elijah stood with the rest of them by the front door to watch Josef drive off with Tyra past the front gates until they had disappeared from sight.

It was a school night, which meant shortly after they had dinner, it was time for Aurora to prepare for bed, which included taking a shower to rinse off the chlorine from the pool water that was beginning to make Aurora's skin itch. Aurora, though, had no clue what to do now that she was Kindred. Luckily, Kiku stepped in and offered to help, much to Nelle's relief, as she did not have the foggiest idea how to wash a Kindred either.

While the two naked Kindred raced up the stairs to head into the washroom, Elijah and Lucas sat with the others in the livingroom where Elijah activated Lucas's tablet so he could check on his emails. He gasped in shock when he recognized the name of the sender of the very first email waiting for him.

"What is it?" Lucas asked, pricking his ears as he looked over at the screen

"It's an email from my father," Elijah said.

He tapped the screen to open the message and began reading it.

From: Erik Saunders
To: Elijah Saunders
Date: Monday, May 23, 2078 at 6:41 PM
Subject: Hello Elijah!

Jonas and I have not heard from you for some time and are quite concerned that you have not written to us or phoned us lately.

Your mother, of course, refuses to discuss with me anything related to your wellbeing. But I had hoped that you would have dropped us a line by now to let us know how you are doing.

Please call me or email me as soon as you get this message to let me know that you are doing fine.

Love, Dad

"I really should call him," Elijah said, inwardly cursing himself for forgetting to even write to his dad.

"It's just after ten now in Ottawa. Do you think that's a little too late to be calling him?" Lucas asked.

Elijah shook his head and smiled knowingly.

"Knowing my dad he's probably staying up late working on some article for the Globe and Mail."

"You could use the phone in dad's office if you'd like some privacy," Lucas suggested.

Elijah nodded his appreciation, but declined, opting instead to just grab the handset from the phone in the main foyer. When he sat back down, he looked over at Lucas as he realized this was going to be a long distance phone call.

Lucas knew his concern, but nodded anyway, assuring him that it was alright. It was, after all, his father he was calling.

Elijah set the phone down on the coffee table, the screen facing him, and listened as it rang once. Then a second time. On the third ring it stopped and he could see the face of his father appear on the screen.

As soon as his father saw his face, he beamed with joy and excitedly called out to Jonas, who came running into the room to see what all the excitement was all about. The huge gorilla stopped and smiled broadly, his nose flaring slightly when he saw Elijah's face on the screen.

"Hi, Dad. Hi, Jonas," Elijah said smiling happily at them both.

SIXTEEN

"Lije, it is so good to see you," Erik said, using the pet name he had given Elijah when he was much younger.

Elijah smiled at his father's use of the name. He actually preferred it over his full name. It brought back many good memories for him, especially the trips to the park when his father would push him on the swings and spin him around on the carousel until he got so dizzy he could barely stand, much less walk straight. Those were the days, carefree and fun.

"I missed you, Dad," Elijah said. "I'm really sorry I haven't written or called lately."

"I understand, with school almost over you must be really busy getting ready for final exams."

"It's not just that, a lot's been happening, some of it bad, but most of it good."

"You're looking much better since the last time I saw you, Elijah. Those retroviral drugs you're receiving must be finally working for you."

Elijah smiled at his father's compliment. But it was only a fleeting smile as he knew he was going to have to tell his father the truth.

"It's not the drugs, Dad. They never worked."

Erik's expression fell.

"I'm sorry, Lije," he said sadly.

Tears stung in Elijah's eyes, knowing that what he was about to say next was really going to hurt his father.

"Dad, I ... I almost died. I wanted to kill myself. I didn't want to die lying in a hospital bed alone. I was going to jump off the New Westminster Bridge and let the river take me instead."

Elijah could see Erik gasp in alarm. Not only him but Jonas as well, who put a steadying hand on his father's shoulder. Erik looked as though he was about to burst into tears.

"I would have been there, Elijah," his father said quietly, using his full name for the first time. "I don't care what that woman would have said, we both would have come."

"I know you would have, Dad. But I also didn't want the frail, sick-looking boy I had become to be your last memory of me. So I couldn't call you."

"It wouldn't have mattered. I would always have the memories of you when you were younger. That's how I always remember you."

Elijah gulped as tears began trickling down his cheeks.

"Mom kicked me out of the house a few weeks ago, Dad. She said she didn't need a dirty, diseased little faggot polluting her house."

Erik's expression changed dramatically as he grew immediately angry.

"That bitch!" he exclaimed, but then quickly covered his mouth as his expression softened. "I'm sorry, I shouldn't have said that."

Elijah laughed, and he could even hear Jonas chuckling quietly in the background.

"Don't worry, Dad, that was mild compared to the things I've been thinking about her recently."

"I always felt that you were gay, even when you were younger."

"Well, maybe a little bi," Elijah admitted, thinking back to his earlier reaction to Kiku out back.

"So if that woman who calls herself your mother kicked you out, where are you staying now? Do you need a place to stay?"

It was then that he suddenly recognized the number displayed at the bottom of the phone's screen

"Wait, why are you calling from Doctor Wolff's home?"

Of course his father would know the doctor. As a political affairs correspondent for the Globe and Mail newspaper, he would have interviewed him lots of times for stories dealing with the Kindred.

Elijah smiled.

"Because that's where I'm staying now," he said, and then quickly added, "with my boyfriend."

"Your boyfriend?" Erik exclaimed excitedly.

Lucas leaned over so that he was visible to Erik and Jonas.

"Hello Mr. Saunders, it's good to see you again," he said.

"Your boyfriend is Lucas Wolff?" Erik said incredulously, a wide smile stretching across his face.

"You lucky dog!" Jonas laughed from behind Erik.

Elijah didn't know if he was referring to him or Lucas, but it did not matter either way, it still made him laugh, and he wholeheartedly agreed with him, too.

Erik playfully elbowed Jonas in the ribs, which only made him laugh even harder.

"I'm so very happy for you, Lije," Erik said. "And Lucas, I hope you're taking good care of my boy."

"I promise you, he's known nothing but love. My dad treats him like a son."

"Dad, it was Lucas who found me on the bridge and stopped me from jumping. He brought me here were his dad helped me. I no longer have AIDS anymore!"

Erik's eyes opened wide with both amazement and relief. If he could have reached out to hug Elijah through the screen, he would have.

"So you're part of the reason why he issued the press release two weeks ago, detailing his intentions to seek funding for research into ridding the world of sexually transmitted diseases."

"That's right," Lucas answered for Elijah. "Since the government was refusing to fund his research he turned to the University instead. They were only too eager to support my dad in any way they could."

Erik nodded thoughtfully.

"And, of course, I have an interview scheduled with your dad for tomorrow."

"I'm looking forward to it, Erik," Per said from behind the couch where Elijah and Lucas were sitting, startling Elijah since he did not even know he was there.

"As am I, Doctor Wolff," Erik said.

"Erik, seeing as how our two boys are now a couple, we can probably dispense with the 'doctor' bit, at least in private, don't you think? The title makes me feel old, and I'm only sixty-seven."

Erik laughed, and nodded in agreement.

"I guess that's true, Per," he said. "Lije, once school is out, Jonas and I would really like it if you, and, of course, Lucas, would come stay with us for a while for a visit."

"I would love to, Dad. The thing is, Josef, a Kindred friend of Lucas's, who's a personal trainer, has agreed to help me work out and get my strength and stamina back so I can hopefully become a lifeguard for the University."

Erik nodded, immediately recognizing the name of the Kindred

"You always were my little tadpole boy," Erik said playfully with a smile.

Lucas snickered while Elijah's face begun to flush red.

"Dad!" Elijah protested, but only halfheartedly. It really did make his heart swell with joy that his father still thought of him that way.

"Don't worry about your training. We have a pool here as well, you know, that you can use, and I'm sure Josef could provide you with a training regimen for you to follow while you're here."

"Or better yet, he could always come with you if he wants," Jonas offered. "There's always room for one more."

"He has a family, though, Jonas. He and his boyfriend have just fostered a young Kindred panther."

"See what he says, Lije. It would be great to interview him as well for a side piece on another article I'm working on."

Elijah nodded enthusiastically.

"I'll see what he says, Dad."

"And don't worry about the cost of the tickets. We'll take care of that once you tell us how many are coming. I know the paper would be willing to cover the expense."

"Can I go, too?" a little voice that entered the room asked.

Elijah looked over where he saw Aurora coming into the living room with Kiku. Both of them had fur that was so shiny and soft looking. Kiku's especially was so radiant that Elijah had difficulty taking his eyes off her.

"Is there room for one more? I'd love to meet your Dad," Kiku said, giggling a little at Elijah's awestruck expression.

"Who's that with you Lije?" Erik asked.

"It's really a full house here, Dad," Elijah explained. "That was Aurora and Kiku. Aurora was just recently made a Kindred because she was sick and it was the only way to make her better. Her parents are here with her too. The other one was Kiku, my friend and classmate from School."

"From the way you were looking, I'd say Kiku is more than just a friend," Erik laughed.

Kiku, of course, heard him and smiled at Elijah, that sparkle in her eye suggesting that she agreed with him.

Elijah met her gaze, and although he was blushing furiously from all of the attention he was getting, much to the amusement of everyone in the room, he could not help but wonder if Lucas had been right all along, that he was attracted to Kiku, even though for most of his life he had always thought of himself as gay. Did he really have room in his heart to love these two beautiful people?

Of course you do, came Lucas's thought.

Elijah knew, as did everyone, that human/Kindred triads were quite common. They were the only polygamous relationships recognized by the government. Most consisted of two Kindred and a human, but some saw two humans joining with a single Kindred instead.

"Mr. Saunders, this is Thomas, Aurora's father."

Elijah turned the phone so that his father could see Thomas sitting with Nelle with Aurora on her lap.

"She's adorable!" Elijah heard Jonas say.

Nelle smiled proudly.

"Thank you, Jonas. We think so, too."

"Hey, you're a gorilla!" Aurora exclaimed with glee.

Jonas laughed.

"That's right."

"It's clear that our daughter is interested in going with Elijah and Lucas. And Nelle and I have no objections, but, of course, we would need to come as well. We could both do with a vacation. Are there any suitable hotels that the two of you could recommend for us?"

"I couldn't recommend any, Thomas, to be perfectly honest. During the summer months, unfortunately, they jack their prices up considerably for the tourist season. Instead we would be honoured if you would consider staying in our little guest house. It easily has enough room to accommodate a small family and the bedrooms all look out onto the lake."

"That's very generous of you, Jonas." He was amazed that someone he had never met before would make such an offer.

"He may be big and hairy, but he's a real softy at heart," Erik kidded, which earned him a playful slap across the back of his head.

Thomas and Nelle laughed.

"What about me?" Kiku asked as she walked into the frame, suddenly feeling left out.

"Provided you have permission from your parents, you could use the spare room in the main house," Erik told her. "Jonas and I kept one bedroom available for Lije if he ever one day came for a visit, so the third one is yours."

It was obvious that Kiku liked the idea. Elijah could tell by the excitement in her eyes. Somehow in those eyes he also saw a hint of mischievousness. The way she was now looking at him made him believe that her bedroom was not where she was thinking of sleeping, or that sleeping was on her mind at all.

Is she going into heat or something?

Not yet, but soon, came the laughing reply in his head.

Elijah turned the phone back so he could see his father.

"It's a school night, Dad, so I'd better say good night and get off the phone so I can get ready for bed."

Erik nodded in agreement.

"Please don't hesitate to call me again, Lije, for anything. This thing with your mother, it's complicated, but you'll be eighteen in a month and so will be an adult and then there is nothing she can say about what you do with your life."

"I will, Dad. I promise," Elijah agreed. "Jonas, you take care of my dad for me."

"You know I will, Elijah. Take care."

"I love you. The both of you," Elijah said.

Erik and Jonas both smiled.

"We love you too, Lije. Good night."

With that the connection closed as Elijah pressed the disconnect button.

"Well, if I'm going to get the chance to come with you this summer to see your dad, I'd better get home so I can talk to my parents."

"Do you think they'll let you come?" Lucas asked.

"Are you kidding?" she asked incredulously. "When I told them that I was friends with you two it's all they can talk about now. I need a vacation away from them as much as I need one from school! They'll let me go, believe me."

"Would you like a lift home, Kiku?" Thomas offered. "You just had a shower and I don't think you want to get all sweaty running home."

"That's nice of you to offer, Mr. Avery, thank you," she said.

Kiku gave Lucas and Elijah both lingering hugs, and a special one to Aurora before she left with Thomas to the car.

"Now, as for the two of you," Per said, looking at Lucas and Elijah. "It's time for you to have a shower and rinse off that chlorine from the pool."

Lucas shook his head as he stood up with Elijah and the two of them obediently headed for the stairs.

"Thirty-two-years-old and he still treats me like a kid," Lucas muttered under his breath.

"I heard that!" Per said from the living room.

Elijah laughed as they climbed the stairs.

SEVENTEEN

Their shower that night was another one of those experiences that Elijah would never forget. After stripping off his clothes while Lucas turned on the water in the shower, getting the temperature of the water just right, he quickly enveloped Elijah in his arms before they even got under the water and proceeded to kiss Elijah with such passion that it made his head spin.

Elijah could feel Lucas's tongue sliding in his mouth and wrapping around his own tongue as he stroked it lovingly back and forth. The sensations he was feeling overwhelmed him, and he was overcome with lust as his arms greedily began holding Lucas closer to him, as though trying to merge their two bodies into one. His hand drifted down to Lucas's tail while Lucas continued to make love to his tongue and he felt the junction where his tail met the furry round cheeks of his butt.

By now they had backed into the shower, somehow managing not to trip over the lip of the shower stall. The hot water fell onto both their bodies, its warmth increasing the passion between them. They were not even concerned with washing. It was the farthest thing from both their minds.

Words were not spoken between them, there was no need. Lucas stopped kissing Elijah and looked lovingly into his brilliant blue eyes before bending over and presenting himself to Elijah for the first time. Elijah moved behind him and stared admiringly at Lucas. Then, in one swift movement, they became one, and Lucas had to stifle a howl of pain and pleasure as he felt Elijah begin to move within him.

Elijah rocked gently back and forth eliciting groans of immense joy and pleasure from Lucas as his fingertips grazed the sensitive side of Lucas's neck and down his sides.

Soft moans filled the room, barely audible over the sound of the running water splashing off their bodies as they moved rhythmically against each other. Elijah made love to his Kindred boyfriend, slowly at first but growing steadily faster as both their passions grew, both of them desperately working their way to that ultimate release.

Elijah had never felt as much love for someone as he did now. As he moved within Lucas, feeling him ripple with pleasure, Elijah's hands moved to Lucas's hips, holding him firmly in place as his movements grew increasingly urgent.

The water was starting to turn cold, but neither of them noticed. They were too far gone in their pleasure to notice anything else around them but the overwhelming sensations they each were feeling.

When Elijah could hold back no more, he thrust one final time, burying himself as deeply within Lucas as he could and suddenly was thrown headlong into the most earth shattering climax he had ever experienced in his young life. At the same time, he could feel Lucas tightening around him as they both amazingly reached their climaxes together.

They stood there, in the aftermath, breathing heavily as they both slowly came down from the rush. Elijah, still buried within Lucas, leaned forward and placed gentle kisses all over Lucas's muscular back.

As they finally separated, Lucas turned and drew Elijah back into another deep kiss. This one still passionate, but more gentle and loving.

It was only then that they both began to realize that they had almost completely run out of hot water. They quickly washed each other off, hurrying before the water became ice cold, and got out of the shower. They each grabbed a towel to dry themselves off.

Back in their room, Elijah had Lucas sit on the bed as he went to the nightstand where he retrieved the brush from the drawer.

"I think I promised you a brushing earlier."

Lucas looked up at him as he approached the bed, and smiled.

For the next half hour, Elijah ran the brush through his fur. His winter coat was now mostly gone, replaced with a shorter, more fine coat of fur. It glowed just like Kiku's did in the light of the room.

Lucas's body vibrated with pleasure each time the brush stroked the fur on his belly, running down to his crotch. And even though they had only recently made love, he could nevertheless feel himself responding to Elijah's ministrations.

Elijah saw this and smiled, wickedly. He put the brush down on the nightstand and gently coaxed Lucas to lean back until he was laying in the centre of the bed. Then, still smiling, he straddled his lover's waist and lowered himself until he felt the pointed tip of Lucas's wet member pressing up against him, poking him between the cheeks of his bum.

But he did not stop there. He kept going until he felt Lucas slip inside him. He stopped for a moment, trying to get used to the feeling of Lucas once again within him, and then slowly, as the shock of his initial entry subsided, continued until Lucas was buried fully within him.

"My turn," Elijah said, with a loving grin.

All Lucas could do was smile and nod ever so slightly.

Elijah began the slow gentle ride over Lucas, feeling him hard and deep within him. Lucas reached up to hold him by the hips, gently coaxing him as they rocked back and forth. Elijah leaned forward, and began a long deep kiss that only inflamed their once again growing passion.

The bed, thankfully, was silent as their bodies moved together in perfect sync. Such was the pleasure he was feeling the Lucas had to place a pillow over his head to muffle out the gasps and moans he was making as he felt Elijah over him, pleasuring him with his hot body. It was as though every muscles of Elijah's was working to give him as much pleasure as he could possibly withstand, and then some.

Both of them were quickly working toward another powerful climax. Elijah's movements over Lucas grew more desperate as he too began panting and moaning with pleasure. And then, he felt it. Lucas's knot breaking through the tight ring of muscles, startling Elijah with the sudden pain of its entry. But soon after he felt nothing but sweet pleasure as he could feel Lucas pulsing within him. It triggered his own climax, long and hard, almost painful, but ultimately very satisfying.

When it was over, Elijah collapsed on top of Lucas. their passions finally sated at last. He had just enough strength left in him to rise up slightly and plant a loving kiss on Lucas's lips.

"I love you, Lucas. So much."

Lucas looked up into Elijah's eyes. He could see the love he felt for him in them. He reached up to softly caress the side of Elijah's face.

"I love you, too, Elijah."

Resting back down on him. Elijah finally started to drift off to sleep, letting the sound of Lucas's strong and steady heartbeat lull him into blissful unconsciousness.

Fifth period English class for Elijah seemed to drag on forever. Every time he looked up at the clock above the door, only minutes had passed instead of the hours that felt like should have. He gave up looking at the clock after the sixth or seventh time, deciding it would only prolong his agony further. And this despite the fact that English was among his best subjects, and most favourite even.

But even the project he was supposed to be working on, a creative writing assignment that the class had been given, something he thoroughly enjoyed normally, could not tear him away from the thoughts that were distracting him, stubbornly occupying his mind like a squatter refusing to leave a home.

His mind was on the other night and the passion he had shared with Lucas, not just once, but twice before they both finally fell asleep. Just the thought of making love to Lucas was having an affect on him, one that he desperately tried to hide from any wandering eyes in the room that might look his way.

He looked down at the page on his desk, and for the umpteenth time stared at the three words he had written down on the piece of paper. They were the only words he had written since they were given the assignment only a half an hour ago by their teacher.

Daring one final look at the clock he saw that there was

only about twelve minutes left before the end of class, and the end of school for the day. Twelve minutes to get something down on paper more substantive than just three simple words. He knew exactly what he wanted to write. It was just a matter of getting the words down on paper before the bell sounded. His hand moved the pencil across the page, furiously scribbling words on the paper in a total blur.

When the bell did go off, it startled him almost out of his seat.

He did not stop, though, not until he finished getting the last sentence of the paragraph he was working on done.

Putting his pencil down, he looked down at his paper, and saw that he had written two whole pages of a story that, in his mind, would make an interesting read one day.

Before the class left, the teacher informed them that for homework they were to finish writing their stories and submit them the next day when their teacher would select the three best stories to be read out loud to the class. There were more than just a few low groans from some of his classmates, most likely from those who did not relish the idea of speaking in front of the whole class. It used to bother Elijah, too, that is, until the day he was called up on stage with Lucas. Now, he did not mind it so much. If he could stand in front of the whole school, then standing in front of just twenty students would be a breeze.

Elijah packed his things in his backpack and joined the crowd of students gathering in the hallways as they headed for their respective lockers.

When he finally walked through the front doors of the school and started home a great smile stretched across his face as he thought of all the things he wanted to do with Lucas when he got home.

But it was because of this that he did not notice the white

van with tinted windows pull up alongside him. Nor did he notice the two men who quietly left the van and sneaked up behind him. Only when he was grabbed from behind, a hand covering his mouth to prevent his startled cry, did he finally realize the danger he was in.

He struggled desperately to escape with all his might, but to no avail. Then, before they dragged him into the back of the van, one of the men placed a wet cloth over his nose and mouth. He could smell the acrid fluid that saturated the cloth and tried to move his face so he could breath. But very quickly he found himself growing weak, and his struggles eventually ceased.

As he began to lose consciousness, he did the only thing he could think of and screamed out to Lucas in his mind for help. There was no way of knowing if Lucas had heard him, though, before everything went black.

Lucas sat in the lounge chair as he waited for Elijah to return from school. Per had already completed his interview with Elijah's father, Erik Saunders from the Globe and Mail about the research he was conducting and the government's angry reaction to the news of what he was doing, and was now in the kitchen preparing for dinner.

He was just about to grab his drink, when all of a sudden he felt a terrible pain in his head that caused him to whimper and fall out of the chair onto the grass. It did not last, however, and as quickly as it hit him it was gone. But just before it disappeared entirely, he thought he heard Elijah's voice calling out to him for help.

Per had obviously heard Lucas's cry of pain and rushed out to see what was the matter. He raced to Lucas, still holding his head.

"Lucas, what's wrong?" Per asked, his concern evident in his voice.

Lucas looked up at him with tears in his eyes. His ears were folded against his skull, showing his distress.

"It's Elijah!" he said with alarm, trying to catch his breath. "They've taken Elijah!"

"Who's taken him, Lucas?" Per asked, now very afraid for Elijah.

Lucas shook his head.

"I don't know, there was a brief flash of pain, and then I heard him cry out to me for help, and then nothing. I can't even sense him at all!"

"Alright, Lucas, we'll figure out what's happened to Elijah. I promise," Per said as he helped Lucas up.

Just then the phone began to ring inside.

Per quickly raced inside with Lucas hot on his heals. He pushed the connect button on the fourth ring.

Although the call was connected, there was no image and no phone number listed on the display.

"Doctor Per Wolff," a voice on the other end of the phone said.

"This is he," Per answered, his tone even though he was as frightened as Lucas was.

"We have Elijah Saunders."

"Who is this?" Lucas demanded impatiently.

"Who we are isn't important. That we have your boyfriend is. And if you ever want to see him again, I suggest you do as we tell you."

"What do you want?" Per asked.

"We want you to reverse everything you did to create the Kindred."

"What?" Per exclaimed with alarm. "It's impossible. It

can't be done!"

"So you say. But we have someone here who says it is possible. You are instructed to within one day come up with a method of reversing the Kindred process. And furthermore, if you make an attempt to contact the authorities, we will know about it and Elijah's life will be forfeit. Do we make ourselves clear, Doctor?"

"Very," Per said, his voice taught with anger.

"Good. We will contact you again tomorrow at this time. Have a nice evening."

The connection died.

"What are we going to do, Dad?" Lucas asked fearfully, tears welling up in his eyes.

"I may have no choice but to comply," Per said with a reluctant sigh.

"But it can't be undone, can it?"

"Not without severely crippling any Kindred who becomes human, or even killing them."

"I don't think these people care about that," Lucas said. His tears gave way to a sudden anger. His lips curled back in a snarl and his tail began thrashing violently from side to side. "Well I'm not going to let them get away with it."

"There's nothing that can be done, though," Per insisted.

"No, you're wrong there, Dad. The Kindred can do what we were created to do in the first place: we can hunt down and eliminate these terrorists. I will make sure they pay for threatening to hurt my boyfriend."

"Who are you calling?" he asked, when Lucas started punching numbers into the phone.

"I'm calling Josef," Lucas said, looking back at his father as he placed the call.

EIGHTEEN

Elijah groggily woke up in a dimly lit, mostly empty room. Every muscle in his body ached and his mouth felt extremely dry. He groaned in discomfort and tried to stretch. That is when he discovered his feet were secured to the legs of the chair he was sitting on and his hands were bound behind his back.

Panicking, he looked around at the room to try and find a way to escape. It's only source of light was a small window near the ceiling, its height from the floor indicating he was probably in a basement, and other than the chair he was sitting in, the only piece of furniture was a wooden table in front of him. One door led into the room, a big heavy steel door. There was no getting through there if it was locked, which Elijah assumed it probably was. The window also was not a viable exit either, as he could clearly see metal bars covering it.

He tried desperately to free his hands from the ropes that bound him, but they were too secure, making his attempts to free himself from them painful as the rope chafed the skin on his wrists.

The lock on the door clicked, and the door swung open. A man walked in that he did not recognize, and behind him and older woman. When the light struck her face he gasped in shock. It was his own mother!

"I see that you're awake," the man sneered, looking down contemptuously at Elijah as he sat on the corner of the table. "You're going to be a guest with us for a while."

"Who are you? Why are you doing this to me?" Elijah rasped painfully, his throat too sore.

"Oh it's not you that we want. Rather it's what your boyfriend's father can do for us that we're interested in. You're just insurance."

"I have no idea what you're talking about."

"No, I suppose you don't," the man nodded. "They've been brainwashing you, son. But we can fix that, make you well again."

"You're nuts," Elijah said, staring at the man incredulously.

That's when his mother stepped forward, and with the back of her hand slapped him hard across his face.

"You will show more respect!" She said angrily.

"Now, now, Meredith. There's no need for violence," the man admonished her, though Elijah did not think he cared one way or the other since he made no attempt to stop her. "We need to help this boy, not hurt him."

"Yes, Reverend."

Lucas, where are you. I need you!

No answer.

"I will leave the two of you alone for a while so you can get reacquainted."

The man stood up, nodded to Meredith, and walked out of the room, closing the door behind him. Elijah heard the click of the lock as it was secured once again.

"Why are you doing this to me?" he asked Meredith.

"It's for your own good, honey. The reverend can help you like he helped me to see the truth."

"What truth is that?"

"That the Kindred are Satan's abomination sent here to corrupt the human race's purity."

Elijah just stared at the woman he used to call mom. He barely recognized her any more. Her eyes were all glassy. She stared at him, but he did not even think she really saw him. She was clearly under the influence of some powerful drug.

Is this the fate that awaits me? he wondered.

Not if I can help it!

Lucas, he heard him! He did not let his excitement on his face show, however, lest his mother became suspicious.

"Mom, that's crazy talk. The Kindred are people, like you and me. They just look different, that's all," Elijah tried reasoning with her. "Doctor Wolff created the Kindred so that they could fight the terrorists."

"Government propaganda, that is all. They told us what we wanted to hear and we fell for it. We accepted the Kindred into our lives and look what's happening now, they're corrupting us. Before they came around, polygamous marriages were illegal!"

"Mom, it doesn't have to be this way. We can leave here, together. You and me."

"We will, honey, once we've gotten what we wanted."

"And what's that?"

"To reverse the process and make the Kindred human again."

Elijah gasped with alarm.

"That'll kill them, mom!" he shouted at her.

"They are better off as dead humans than Kindred abominations, Elijah," she said with conviction. Her eyes, however, were still blank, and he did not know whether it was really her talking or the drugs that she had obviously been given. "I'll leave you now to think about it. I'm sure once you've had a chance to talk to the Reverend, you'll come around too."

She turned and left, knocking on the door to be let out of the room. Once the door closed again, leaving him very alone, and very frightened.

We're coming, Lije. Don't worry! Can you describe where you are?

I'm in a basement some place, with a big metal door and bars on the window.

Can you move to the window to look outside?

Maybe, but I'm tied to a chair.

Try as he might, though, he was unable to free his legs from the chair at all, and he was so sore and tired that the attempt left him completely breathless. He just wanted to sleep.

No, stay awake! he heard Lucas tell him.

Through sheer force of will, Elijah was able to keep his eyes open, but only just. Then, he had an idea. As carefully as he could he began to stand up. The chair made it impossible for him to stand upright, but it was enough that he was able to shuffle painfully towards the window.

He could not quite see out the window. It was still too high. He needed to stand up straighter.

Try to work the bonds up the leg of the chair, Lucas suggested.

Although the ropes that held his feet were secure, they were not so tight that he could not move his legs at all. Slowly, one inch at a time, he was able to inch his way up the legs, allowing him to stand straighter. He was now eye level with the window and could just make out some of the building outside.

I'm in some kind of industrial complex. It looks empty. A lot of the buildings look really run down. There's a sign on one of the buildings. It reads Canwest something. I can only make out part of it.

I think I know the place. There's an old abandoned factory just on the edge of Surrey. It's going to take a little time, but we're coming.

Please hurry, Lucas. My mom is here and they've been using some kind of drug on her. She looks more like a zombie now than she does my mother.

Might be a psychotropic drug she's been given. It could explain her sudden behaviour towards you and the Kindred.

I think they're going to try and use it on me.

Not going to happen! Lucas assured him. *Sit tight. We're coming.*

Elijah struggled, but was eventually able to return to the table and to sit down exactly where he had been before. He hoped that if they did notice he had moved, that they would just assume he had been trying to escape.

He was still very much afraid, but he felt a little better now that Lucas would find him. He just hoped he would not be too late.

When Josef arrived at the house, Lucas was waiting for him at the front door.

Josef stepped out of his car and hurried to him. From his demeanour, Lucas knew the old soldier had returned.

"I'm so sorry, Lucas," Josef said, embracing him

warmly.

"We're getting him back," Lucas said matter of factly.

"You're damn right we are," Josef agreed. "The moment you called me to tell me that Elijah had been kidnapped, I contacted the old squad. They should be arriving shortly."

No sooner had Josef spoken than several cars pulled into the driveway. In each of the cars were several Kindred. All of them the original members of Josef's squad who Lucas immediately recognized.

"Thank you all for coming. Please follow me, there's been some new developments," Lucas said.

He led the group into Per's office, where Per was seated at his desk tapping commands into his tablet.

Per looked at them as they entered his office, and nodded.

"I wish we were all meeting again under better circumstances, gentlemen, but as I'm sure Josef has told you there is a situation that has come up that demands immediate attention.

"Josef told us that Lucas's boyfriend was kidnapped by some group demanding that you reverse the process that made us Kindred," a lion said.

"That is correct, Dax," Per nodded. "What you haven't been told, though, is that for some reason Lucas and Elijah have developed a telepathic bond that has enabled them to communicate with each other—even over great distances—without anyone being the wiser."

"Have you been talking to Elijah since his disappearance, Lucas?" a gorilla asked.

"I have, Ulrik. He has been able to give me a rough idea of where he is located."

Per activated the three-dimensional monitor on his desk

and an image appeared over it.

"This is the old, abandoned Canwest Tanks and Ecological Systems plant just on the edge of town. Based on Elijah's description, this is where he's being held."

"Do we know who we're dealing with?" a cougar asked.

"Given that there were multiple references of someone named 'Reverend' I can only guess that we're dealing with a group of religious fanatics."

"Terrorists," spat a wolf derisively.

Per nodded in agreement.

"We can't involve the police or the military for this. They have threatened to kill Elijah if we do," Lucas said.

"When do we go in?" Ulrik asked, cracking the knuckles in his impressively massive hands in anticipation of the coming battle.

"At nightfall," Josef answered.

"Just one thing," Lucas said, getting their attention once again. "I'm going in with you."

Josef wanted to say something to dissuade him, but the look Lucas gave him suggested it would be a futile effort. Whether he went with them or followed after them, he was going regardless. He nodded at Lucas reluctantly.

"Just don't take any unnecessary risks, Lucas," Josef cautioned him. "You may have had some hand to hand combat training before, but you're not a soldier."

Night had fallen.

The tiny window that once provided the only source of light in the room Elijah was in was dark. Not even the moonlight shawn in through the window. He was left in almost total darkness.

His wrists and ankles hurt from being tied up for so long. His leg had seized up in a cramp at least twice, but there was nothing he could do to alleviate the pain.

He felt lightheaded, and his thoughts were confused. Sometime during the day the person his mother had referred to as the Reverend came in with a hypodermic needle. Elijah struggled in a vain attempt to prevent himself from being injected by whatever was in the needle, but tied up as he was there was no escape. The Reverend left soon after, a wry grin forming on his face after Elijah settled down and then became unconscious.

He did not know how long he was out for, but he did know it was night. He also knew he had to pee really bad. His captors, though, had not shown any interest in allowing him to see to his personal needs. As time went by his need became increasingly urgent, until he could hold it in no longer and released his bladder.

The room, which was quite warm, despite the cool evening air outside, now stunk of urine. But there was nothing Elijah could do about it. He only hoped that Lucas would find him soon.

A shadow flew across the window, catching Elijah's attention suddenly. Then another. There was definitely something out there. But he could hear no sound. Whatever it was, it was very quiet.

Then, from outside his room, he could hear the shouts of men and women as they moved past the door. No one came in, though. Until, that is, his mother entered the room. She had a look on her face that was almost indescribable. Anger, confusion, and then fear washed across her face in rapid succession as she stepped into the room, closing the door behind her silently.

At first, Elijah thought she was here to finally help him. Perhaps she had somehow managed to break free of the control the Reverend had over her. But that was not the case, he saw, as she withdrew a gun from her pocket and pointed it at him.

"What have you done?" she hissed angrily.

"I don't know what you're talking about," Elijah said, slurring his words, as he was still under the influence of whatever it was the Reverend had injected him with.

"Kindred are swarming this place like locusts. They're killing my brothers and sisters!" She advanced forward, hitting him across the side of the head with the gun, stunning Elijah. "What did you do?"

Elijah, still reeling from the blow to his head, the force of which caused a ringing in his ears, and he could feel blood trickling down from a gash on his temple, stared up at her with fear in his eyes.

She's here to kill me, he thought.

He decided on taking the only course of action available to him. He told her the truth.

"The next time you kidnap someone, make sure it's someone who's not a telepath."

This caused her to pause, her anger momentarily vanishing and a look of shock flashing across her face.

"You're lying."

"I've been trapped here in this chair for God knows how long, a chair that you put me in. Your 'Reverend' has injected me with something, and you expect I'd just sit here like a good little boy and not try anything to escape?" He almost laughed. "Lucas and the original team of Kindred soldiers are out there right now doing what they were trained to do since they became Kindred. They're dealing with a group of terrorists."

"We're not terrorists!" his mother exclaimed angrily,

raising her hand as if to strike him again, but then thought better of it "We're trying to save humanity."

"By kidnapping children, threatening to kill them, and working to kill hundreds, if not thousand, more people. That makes you a terrorist, Mom."

"No," she said quietly, her hand with the gun lowering slightly.

Elijah could see a flicker of doubt in his mother's eyes.

"Mom, listen to me. You're being used. The Reverend has given you drugs that have made you susceptible to suggestion. I know this isn't you."

She did not move, but continued staring at him.

"Remember the fun times we used to have when I was a kid? Remember the trips to the park you used to take me on with dad? Remember holding me while we lay in bed and you read to me my favourite stories before going to sleep?"

"Elijah?" There were tears in her eyes.

"Those are the memories I have of you, Mom. I wish it could be that way again. It can be, if you would only help me."

"I can't," she said quietly, shaking her head.

The conflict within her was growing, Elijah could see that. No matter what drugs or methods of persuasion the Reverend had used on her all these years, there was little that could ultimately break the bonds between a mother and her child. Somehow, deep inside, that part of her still remained and was now struggling to come back

Just then a man ran into the room. It was the Reverend. His face was twisted in anger as he stared at Elijah.

"Kill him now, Meredith!" he spat angrily.

But Meredith hesitated. She turned to face the Reverend and shook her head.

"I can't," she said. "He's my son."

The Reverend scowled at her and advanced on her, striking a blow to her face and grabbing the gun from her hands. She fell to the floor in a crumpled heap, stunned by the blow. He smiled viciously at Elijah.

"Your boyfriend may have found out where we are, but he'll be too late to save you."

"No!" Meredith exclaimed weakly.

Somehow she managed to recover enough to get up and began struggling with the Reverend for control of the gun.

Out of the corner of his eye Elijah saw Lucas, in a snarling rage, appear at the door way.

Just then a shot rang out, its sound painfully echoing off the walls in the almost empty room. Then Elijah felt the stabbing pain in his abdomen, and a wetness grow under his shirt. He looked down, and from the light cast on his from the open doorway saw that his shirt was covered in blood. His blood.

The last thing he saw before passing out was Lucas charging into the room, heading straight for the now terrified Reverend, and hearing the Reverend's screams as Lucas tore into the man. The screaming finally stopped, but so too did everything else.

NINETEEN

The sounds of electronic devices beeping at regular, steady intervals, timed almost perfectly with the beating of his own heart, echoed in Elijah's ears as he slowy regained consciousness,

He could hear voices, also, surrounding him. But he could not see the people, or quite make out what they were saying. Their voices sounded muffled, as though their voices came from under water.

He could feel that he was laying on a bed, the smell of sterile sheets filling his nose, almost making him sneeze.

He discovered also, to his alarm, that he could not see. Everything was black. But then he realized his eyes were closed, and he relaxed. Slowly he tried to open them. Bright light flooded his eyes painfully. He blinked against it, trying to adjust to the light.

That's when he saw them, Lucas and Per, Josef, his mother and father, Jonas and even Kiku, all huddled around him.

He smiled.

"Lije!" Lucas said, his voice ecstatic and filled with relief as he saw him wake up. He carefully covered Elijah's body with his and cried happily.

"I like it when you call me that," Elijah croaked. His throat still hurt. "Where am I?"

Per poured a glass of water for him, which he gladly accepted and drank. It helped to relieve some of the scratchiness.

"You're at Surrey Memorial Hospital," Per said. "You were in surgery for quite some time. The Doctors almost lost you twice on the table."

Elijah frowned. Suddenly it all came back to him, his mother struggling with the Reverend, the sound of the gun going off, and then the pain he felt in his stomach. He had been shot. He put his hand to his stomach but strangely he could not feel it. At all. In fact, he could feel nothing below his stomach. His eyes opened wide with alarm.

"I'm sorry I couldn't get to you in time, Elijah. The bullet severed your spinal cord" Lucas told him, seeing his distress.

"I-I'm paralyzed?" he asked fearfully.

Tears filled his eyes as he suddenly realized all his hopes and dreams of getting back into shape, swimming again, and becoming a lifeguard, they were dreams that he could never fulfill.

"I'm so, so sorry, Elijah. I didn't want any of this to happen. I swear," his mother said, her head bowed, unable to look at him.

"I'm afraid so, Lije," his father said quietly.

Elijah could tell his father wanted to pick him up and hold him in his arms to make it all better. But that was impossible.

"What am I going to do now?" he asked quietly.

"The doctors say there is nothing more they can do. They've repaired the damage as best they could, and you're going to make an otherwise full recovery. But there's nothing they can do to repair the spinal cord."

"So I'm going to be stuck in a wheelchair for the rest of my life."

"No, Lije, I don't want that to happen to you, there is another way, tell him, Dad," Lucas said.

"It's too risky, Lucas, I told you that," Per replied.

"Look at him, Dad. He's right back where he started, where I found him, in a desperate situation, with no hope of ever getting better. Just look into his eyes and tell me he wouldn't rather die than to live like that."

Lucas was right, Elijah knew. He would rather die than become an invalid, always having to be waited on and cared for by others. Never again would he feel the pleasures of Lucas's fur rubbing up against him, of feeling Lucas's love deep inside him. It would be worse than death.

"Please tell me, Doc, I don't want to live like this," Elijah pleaded with Per, desperate tears running down the side of his face.

"There are two options possible," Per said with a reluctant sigh. "The first is that I could create a series of nanobots that would form a permanent bridge between the two severed ends of your spinal cord. They would act as a conduit allowing the signals from your brain to reach your lower extremities."

"What's the catch?" Erik asked.

"While Elijah would regain sensation in his lower abdomen and legs again, the nanobots alone would be insufficient to allow him full motor control. You might walk again, Elijah, but only for short distances, and even then you would need a walker to maintain your balance."

Elijah did not particularly like that idea. It was better than the situation he currently found himself in, but it would still rob him of his independence and his ability to do what he loved most.

"What's the other option?" he asked.

"This last option, while less risky, is quite drastic," Per cautioned. "You could become Kindred."

For a moment Elijah stared at Per, at first, not believing what he was hearing. To become a Kindred...

"How will that help, Elijah?" Meredith asked, looking up at Per. "His spinal cord would still be damaged."

Per shook his head.

"Part of the process of becoming a Kindred involves stimulating certain stem cells within the body. Once these stem cells have been reprogrammed by my nanobots, and placed strategically throughout the body, they start developing into new tissues, and in some cases new organs. Some of the original Kindred were people who were missing limbs. Those limbs grew back again."

"It does sound a better alternative than the first option, and definitely better than remaining like this for the rest of my life," Elijah admitted.

"If you decide to do this, Elijah, the only thing you would need to decide is what kind of Kindred you would like to be," Lucas said, smiling at him.

Elijah did not have to think about it, though. He knew already. He had privately fantasized about it enough times.

"Where are my things? From the house I mean," he asked.

"In here, Lije," Lucas said, walking to a closet. He

opened the door and removed his duffle bag from inside. "What would you like me to get for you?"

"Look inside for a thick red folder."

"Okay, I've got it," Lucas said, holding it up.

"Go ahead and open it up," Elijah suggested with a smile.

Lucas took the folder and opened it up to the first page, he was shocked to discover what was inside.

"You were writing a book?" he asked.

Elijah nodded and Erik chuckled.

Like father, like son, Erik thought.

"Read the synopsis at the front," Elijah said.

Lucas did, and his eyes became wide with surprise.

"You wrote a book about a boy who becomes a Kindred?"

"I started writing it when I first discovered I had AIDS. I've never shown this story to anyone, though. Not even my dad."

Lucas began skimming through each page, and each time discovering something new about his boyfriend.

"You were the boy in the story. You wanted to become Kindred," Lucas said.

"For the longest time I thought how cool it would be to be a wolf. And then later when I saw Josef, and saw how beautiful his black fur looked, I changed the story a bit so that the wolf the boy became was as black as midnight."

"You want to be this boy. You want to be the black wolf?" Lucas asked.

Elijah nodded, smiling at Lucas.

"If becoming a Kindred is the only way I'll be able to walk again, then that's what I'd like to be."

Per put a comforting hand on his arm, the one not

connected to an intravenous line.

"If you are sure, I can start making the preparations as soon as the doctors here say you're well enough to be released.

"I'm well enough now," Elijah insisted.

Erik chuckled.

"I know how anxious you are to get out of the hospital, Lije, but you need to give your body time enough to heal. you don't want to pull out your stitches and wind up right back here again do you?

"No, I guess not," Elijah said with a resigned sigh.

"So, did you have a picture of the wolf?" Kiku asked. She was looking over Lucas's shoulder at the story as he continued to flip through the pages.

Again Elijah nodded. He had Lucas turn to the last page where he had taped to the back a photograph of a majestic black wolf standing on some rocks.

"I know that picture!" Meredith said.

"It's the picture you took, Mom, the last time we went to the Kamloops Wildlife Park together. You, me and Dad."

"You've kept this all this time?" she asked with sadness in her eyes.

"I told you I had lots of good memories of us when we were together."

Elijah was released from the hospital two days later. Thanks to the medications they gave him intravenously, his recovery was much farther along than it normally would if he had been left to his own devices to heal. The stitches had naturally dissolved, leaving behind a long red scar where they had to open him up to perform the surgery that saved his live. Still, there was nothing they could do for his spinal cord.

As he was being wheeled out of the hospital by Lucas, the doctor wished him well and handed Erik, who had stayed with him and Lucas the whole time he was in the hospital, a prescription for painkillers, as well as an appointment for him to see a physical therapist to help him for when he emerged from the maturation chamber. The hospital had been made aware of his desire to be Kindred, and approved the treatment Per had offered him.

Funny enough, the physical therapist he had been assigned to visit was none other than Jonas, his father's boyfriend. He figured his father probably had something to do with that. The only problem with that was it would require him to move to Ottawa. He did not mind that so much, but he also did not want to leave behind Lucas or Kiku. They both assured him, however, that they would go wherever he went, and Per actually expressed relief that now he might actually get some peace and quiet. This made Elijah laugh, though only briefly because of the pain.

Before he was carefully loaded into the taxi van waiting for them by Lucas, and his wheelchair folded up and secured in the trunk, Kiku, leaned down to give him a kiss on his cheek. Elijah, though, had other ideas. He moved his face so that when her lips touched him, they connected with his lips instead. For a moment she was stunned, not expecting that he would kiss her in such an intimate way, but very quickly she relaxed into it and enjoyed it.

Will you be mine?

She jerked back in sudden shock. Did he just speak to her in her mind?

Yes, came the reply. *So will you?*

You're asking me to be your girlfriend?

Elijah nodded.

But what about Lucas?

There's room in both of our hearts to love you as well, if you'll have us.

This time it was Lucas talking to her. She was confused. Up to this point she thought they were both exclusively gay, even though she caught them both staring when she teased them a bit. Neither of them had expressed an interest in her other than as friends.

She did not have to spend one minute thinking about it, though. She knew what she wanted. Without hesitation she gave them their answer.

"Yes!" she said aloud.

Wrapped her arms around Elijah, this time giving him the passionate kiss she had always wanted to. Then, standing back up, she faced Lucas and did the same with him. She was not in the least bit surprised that he returned her embrace and her kiss with just as much enthusiasm and passion as she did.

Jonas chuckled from inside the taxi.

"I think a triad has just been born," he said.

Erik, still standing outside, heard his boyfriend and nodded in agreement.

"Once Elijah becomes Kindred, I think it'll actually be the first triad consisting entirely of Kindred."

"Erik, I hope you are prepared for Kindred pups running around your home, because that's what you'll end up with eventually," Per warned him.

Elijah blushed redder than he had ever blushed before. Both Lucas's and Kiku's ears folded back slightly in embarrassment.

"It's a little early to be thinking about kids, Dad, don't you think?" Lucas asked.

"Ask her when she goes into heat," Per said, climbing

into the taxi.

Lucas shrugged his shoulders.

"What happens, happens, I guess. I know Elijah has really wanted to be a father one day."

Kiku looked down at Elijah in surprise.

"He's right. I've always wanted to have children of my own, ever since I was little. I wanted to have the same kind of experience with my children that my parents had with me.

Kiku smiled.

"You never know, Elijah. Like Lucas said, whatever happens, happens."

Her smile and her little suggestive wink had an immediate effect on Elijah, whose shorts tightened as a tent formed. He did not mind except he could not feel it to enjoy it.

After they had all entered the taxi, which was large enough to easily accommodate them all, and not make Elijah feel squashed in one of the rows of back seats where he sat between Lucas and Kiku, they pulled out of the parking lot and headed home.

Elijah's only regret about being made into a Kindred was that his mother would not be around to see him change.

Shortly after she had left the hospital the day he woke up again, she had voluntarily submitted herself before the courts where she pleaded guilty to the charges of kidnapping, forcible confinement and making terrorist threats. She was immediately remanded into custody to await sentencing. Now that it was known that she was largely under the influence of a psychotropic drug, and was manipulated and controlled by the person calling himself the Reverend, however, her lawyers assured them that any sentence she would receive would be relatively light. She was ultimately sentenced to a year in prison and five years probation. Which meant she would likely only be in prison for between six to eight months at most.

At least, Elijah thought, she would get to see the Kindred I will become, and have the chance to be a mother again. Even his dad had managed to forgive her. Although the love between them was long since gone, he would welcome her back into his home so that she could be with Elijah.

The Reverend and most of the other members of his cult were either dead or captured. Those who were captured had sustained serious injuries as a result of the attack on the factory by the Kindred. Several of them had threatened to sue, but when they were told that the Kindred who carried out the raid were technically still under government mandate to deal with terrorist threats, they quickly realized that any hope of winning such a case would be remote.

Elijah was just glad that the man who had started all of this, was dead, killed at the hands of Lucas. He knew it had to have affected him greatly. Lucas had never taken the life of any living thing ever. But he didn't want to press him on it either, for fear that it might be too soon for him to deal with, yet. When the time was right, he knew Lucas would want to talk about it. Until then, he planned to be the best boyfriend to both him and Kiku he possibly could.

The taxi pulled into the driveway, creeping past the front gate and then stopped in front of the front doors.

Lucas was the first to jump out of the taxi, already heading for the trunk so he could get out Elijah's wheelchair. He and Kiku both then helped Elijah out of the car, and together they rolled him up to the front doors, which Lucas opened to let them in.

Per paid for the taxi while Erik, Josef and Jonas carried their bags into the house.

"First thing's first, Elijah, before you go into the

chamber, you need to take a shower," he said.

Elijah nodded in understanding. He looked over at Kiku who was giggling a little. He knew without a doubt that she was looking forward to helping him.

The house had no elevator, so Lucas had to carry Elijah up the stairs while Kiku folded the wheelchair and brought it up as well. Pretty soon the three of them disappeared into the washroom together.

His shower was uneventful, except for Kiku's lingering touch as she scrubbed his naked body down while Lucas held him up for her. Again Elijah found himself responding to her touch, but like before, he still felt nothing. Kiku seemed to understand this, so she did not try to tease him about it. There would be plenty of time for them to really get to know each other after he had become Kindred.

They rolled him out of the washroom, rinsed, dried and naked, down the hall to the lab where Per was waiting with Erik, Jonas and Josef.

"Everything is all set now, Elijah. When you go in, you'll be fast asleep, so you won't feel a thing. I've taken precautions to make sure your IV line can't get tangled like the last time," Per told him.

Elijah nodded in understanding, thankful that Per had remembered that little detail.

"Until your spinal cord has grown back, which I'll know from watching the monitors, I'll be keeping the dosage of pain medication to a minimum. It'll help make the process go more quickly that way."

"Are you ready, Lije?" Erik asked.

Elijah nodded, and smiled up at his father.

Erik carefully lifted him out of the chair and held him while Per placed the rebreather over Elijah's face and carefully inserted the intravenous line to his arm. Then, as Kiku and Lucas both leaped to the top of the chamber and opened the lid, Erik carefully handed him up to them.

Already Elijah was feeling the effects of the sedative flowing into his arm. By the time Kiku and Lucas had gently slipped him into the chamber and closed the lid, Elijah was already fast asleep.

Kiku and Lucas then jumped back down and stared at Elijah floating in the tank.

Lucas moved toward it and put his hand against the glass.

"I'll see you soon, Lije," he said quietly.

ABOUT THE AUTHOR

Jason Finigan was born in Bracebridge, Ontario in 1973 and was raised in Burlington, Ontario by his adoptive parents. At the age of seventeen, he graduated from Lord Elgin High School. As an avid science-fiction fan growing up, Jason immersed himself fully in the genre, watching series such as Doctor Who and Star Trek on TV as often as he could, as well as collecting and reading as many science-fiction novels as he could get his hands on—many of which he still has to this day. He was in fact so fascinated with the genre that he began writing his own science-fiction short stories while in elementary school, many of which earned him high praise from his teachers. In March of 2007, Jason began work on his first science-fiction novel, Destiny's Edge. He currently lives in Toronto, Ontario